Instead of having Sherra arrested, Brody would be better off ensuring that she kept quiet while this mission continued, or his undercover identity would be put even more at risk.

But her digging so far, even if caught only by the good guys—which was doubtful—had potential consequences far beyond Brody's own health. Especially for the lovely Sherra.

He couldn't help thinking about last night. Having her in his arms again.

Making love with her.

His body started to react. If he could have, he would have taken a cold shower right there. Instead, he did the next best thing.

He focused on the danger she had put them all in. Put herself in.

No matter. Despite his anger with what she'd done, he would keep her safe while he got things turned around so he could get back to work—and get his real job finished.

Dear Reader,

Some mysteries are meant to be solved. Others aren't.

The background of *Undercover Soldier* is very loosely based on a mystery in my own life that will never get solved. I've stopped looking for a solution. But that doesn't keep my imagination from working on it....

I hope you enjoy *Undercover Soldier.* It's my first Harlequin Romantic Suspense! Please come visit me at my website, www.LindaOJohnston.com, and at my blog, KillerHobbies.blogspot.com.

And, yes, I'm on Facebook, too.

Linda O. Johnston

LINDA
O. JOHNSTON

Undercover Soldier

ROMANTIC

SUSPENSE

Recycling programs
for this product may
not exist in your area.

ISBN-13: 978-0-373-27784-1

UNDERCOVER SOLDIER

Printed in U.S.A.

LINDA O. JOHNSTON

loves to write. More than one genre at a time? That's part of the fun. While honing her writing skills, she started working in advertising and public relations, then became a lawyer…and still enjoys writing contracts. Linda's first published fiction novel appeared in *Ellery Queen's Mystery Magazine* and won a Robert L. Fish Memorial Award for Best First Mystery Short Story of the Year. It was the beginning of her versatile fiction-writing career. Linda now spends most of her time creating memorable tales of paranormal romance and mystery.

Linda lives in the Hollywood Hills with her husband and two Cavalier King Charles spaniels. Visit her at her website, www.LindaOJohnston.com.

This book is dedicated to everyone who has lost,
or lost track of, someone important in their past.

It's also dedicated to everyone whose present makes those
past relationships...well, a thing of the past.

I'd also like to thank my wonderful agent, Paige Wheeler,
for continuing to inspire me in my writing career and helping
it to flourish, and I'd also like to thank my delightful and
versatile editor, Allison Lyons, who helps and encourages me
no matter which Harlequin series I'm writing for!

And, as always, I dedicate this Harlequin Romantic Suspense
book to my incredible husband, Fred. Our romance is always
filled with suspense...of the best kind!

Chapter 1

Would she figure it out tonight?

Unlikely. She'd tried before. But at least here, at home, Sherra Alexander had no distractions as she did at work. Which was a good thing, considering the nonstandard way she was conducting her research.

Unlocking the door to her condo, she hurried down the dimly lit hallway to her kitchen. She'd bought dinner on her way home to avoid taking time to prepare anything. For the moment, she placed the paper bag containing her food on the small table in the room's center.

Her thoughts remained on the information she'd unearthed that day. This wasn't the first time she had found anomalies, but they were getting odder. More interesting. More puzzling.

What did they really mean?

As she inhaled the aroma of the turkey burger in the

bag, her stomach rumbled. She had worked straight through lunch. She was hungry.

And exhausted.

She'd rest soon. But not yet. For now, she put her handbag onto the seat of a chair, hung her suit jacket on the back and stepped out of her uncomfortable spike-heeled shoes. She sighed as her bare feet rested solidly on the warm linoleum floor.

She prepared to grab a small glass of white wine and take it, along with her dinner, into her office so she could get back to her mission at her computer. But—

She inhaled rapidly and froze. What was that?

She had heard a sound. From somewhere in her apartment?

Holding her breath, she listened. But all she heard now were muted voices from downstairs—her neighbor's two kids, squabbling as usual.

She shook her head. She was just tired. Drained. That happened a lot, thanks to the intensity of her work as an information technology expert for CMHealthfoods, one of the most successful manufacturers of wholegrain breads and cereals. For more than eight hours a day, she searched global databases for information on products, inventory and sales that affected both her company and its competitors. She usually loved it, basked in her daily successes, made it clear to her bosses that she'd take on the most complex assignments.

But right now her personal online search absorbed her even more. Worse, it was triggering her imagination— wasn't it?

She noticed then how stuffy her apartment felt for late spring in Bethesda, Maryland. Crossing the room, she peered out the sliding glass door toward the balcony off the kitchen. Most apartments in the residential buildings beyond were well lit, since it was late. Sherra saw nothing unusual. Even so, she grew still again, listening.

There were no sounds now except for the neighbors and the traffic below. She nevertheless decided not to open the door to let air in through the screen. Sure, she felt spooked. What she'd been doing lately made her justifiably nervous.

She pulled a bottle of Chablis from the fridge and poured the glass she had promised herself. She took a sip of the cold, bracing liquid, savored the feeling of it going down her throat. Okay. Enough fooling around.

She grabbed flatware from a drawer, picked up the bag containing her dinner and pulled a thumb drive from her purse. Hands full, she headed down the tiny hall to the small bedroom she used as an office.

And stopped. The door was closed. Had she shut it today? She always left it open.

Well, she must have closed it this morning. No one but she could have been here. If the condo association had sent in someone to do maintenance they'd have given her notice.

Despite her unease, a minor change to her routine like this was no big deal. Usually, she'd have thought nothing of it.

But her recent research had put her on edge.

Maybe she should check things out, just in case. She put the fork she held into the bag, then set it and the glass of wine on the hallway floor near the wall. Still holding the knife, she turned the knob and pushed open the door.

And screamed. Or would have, if one hand hadn't been slapped immediately over her mouth as another grabbed the arm in which she held the knife and wrested it from her.

"Calm down," ordered the man who'd grabbed her. "It's okay." He stood off to her side.

Gasping in terror, she managed to yank herself free and dash back into the kitchen. He was faster. She saw his figure whip by her, blocking her from leaving the kitchen and getting to someplace safe.

A weapon! She needed something to protect herself.

She ran toward the drawer from which she'd gotten the first knife and grabbed a second one.

Only then did she pivot to face him, shoulders hunched, the knife poised in her hand as she prepared to lunge. Instead, she released a gasping moan as he snared her arm.

"Hello, Sherra," said Brody McAndrews.

"Brody." His name sounded like a furious oath emanating from her lovely, full lips. "How did you get into my apartment? You're supposed to be dead."

He expelled a brief ironic laugh. "Yeah. I am." She didn't know the half of it. But that was why he had come.

He continued to grip Sherra's right arm to keep her from stabbing him. The knife she held resembled the first one, which he'd slipped carefully into his back pocket.

"But I... Why are you here?" she demanded.

Good question. He had the answer but couldn't tell her. Not all of it, at least.

Brody had known this wouldn't go well. He had also known he had little choice. Contacting Sherra through usual ways could blow his cover. If it wasn't already blown, thanks to her.

Her damned interference could cost him. A lot. Not to mention the level of danger she could put herself in. And him. And others, too.

"We need to talk," he said. Watchful, he allowed her to keep hold of the knife, knowing it probably gave her a sense of security—a false one. He'd remove it from her soon. Otherwise, she'd undoubtedly use it against him.

"That's for sure," she responded.

He stared at her, breathing deeply to remain in control as he decided how best to play this.

Absorbed in his search on her computer, he hadn't been waiting near her front door as he'd intended. Mistake? Maybe—and he knew better than to make mistakes. Under other circumstances, it could be fatal. It wouldn't happen again.

When he'd heard her arrive, he had waited. If she hadn't come into her office, he'd have easily tracked her down in her apartment, but she had acted as anticipated.

It was time. He darted sideways before she could react, grabbed her from behind and pulled this knife from her grasp, too. But he was suddenly much too aware of the warmth of her body. Its softness.

The memories of how it had felt to make love with her.

"Let me go." She turned in his grasp. "You're hurting me. I'm not going to stab you… Are you going to hurt me, Brody?"

He realized then that his grip had tightened. Slowly, almost mesmerized by her nearness, he had been leaning closer, as if he was going to kiss her the way he used to.

Instead, he abruptly obeyed, releasing her.

She, in turn, backed away quickly, as if she feared his presence. Not surprising. Even so, he despised the pangs of regret and pain that shot through him. He shrugged them off.

She bumped into a chair pushed beneath the small kitchen table. That stopped her retreat, but he saw her glance toward the door leading out of the kitchen. She wanted to flee.

He couldn't let her.

"We need to talk," he repeated. "Give me a few minutes so I can tell you why I'm here."

He watched emotions sweep over her lovely face. She'd never been able to hide her feelings from him. He just watched as she mulled over what he'd said. Enjoying the view despite himself.

Sherra was as beautiful as she'd been when they were together. Maybe even more so. Her face was oval, her skin still smooth and perfect. Her nose was a bit long, and her deep brown eyes were underscored by prominent cheekbones.

Her hair was different, though. Years ago, when they'd been together, she had kept it trimmed in a shoulder-length cap of gleaming black. Now, it was longer and straight, draping below the top of her dressy white blouse. She looked businesslike, but her beauty wasn't minimized by her capable appearance.

He hadn't imagined a techie dressing so professionally, but it made sense. She worked for a major corporation.

So did he—sort of. Two of them. Right now he had on jeans and a T-shirt, instead of the slightly dressier civilian stuff he wore to the place where he worked undercover.

For now, at least. Assuming she hadn't ruined his assignment. He continued to hold his temper in check. Getting upset wouldn't resolve anything.

"Why don't I make us a pot of coffee?" she said.

He could have used something stronger—stronger, even, than the glass of wine that sat on the hall floor—but caffeine would do. "Sounds good."

This time when he approached the open doorway leading to the hall out of her apartment, he ambled casually. He crossed his arms and leaned against the wall, blocking her exit—and feeling the weight of both knives in his back pocket. Fortunately, neither looked sharp enough to slice through his slacks, but he'd discard them soon. He hadn't brought the gun he usually carried. Despite what Sherra had done to him by her hacking, he had no intention of harming her.

She shot him a knowing yet irritated smile. "Don't worry. I'm not running away. Not till I get some answers."

Some answers. That was the key. He would tell her just enough to get her to listen. To do as he said.

"Fine."

Brody.

Sherra wanted to scream at him.

Or laugh—in relief?

Instead of doing either, she walked purposefully toward the refrigerator. He again stood between her and the main exit. What would happen if she ran out onto the balcony across the room and screamed for help? Probably nothing helpful—at least not fast enough.

The smart phone she used was in her purse, and that remained on the chair.

For now she'd make coffee, though she might feel better drinking a serious amount of wine. She extracted a packet from the freezer, filled a carafe with water and got the expensive machine on the counter ready to brew. The strong scent of coffee soon filled the kitchen.

"It'll be a few minutes," she said. "Have a seat." She removed her purse from the chair and placed it on the edge of the tile counter near the coffeemaker. With her back toward Brody, she managed to extract her phone, but she had no pockets in her slender suit skirt. She just put it on the counter and set her purse on top of it. For now.

Then she turned and looked at him.

His face was just as she remembered, all masculine and angular, his amber-colored eyes deep set beneath thick brows. They were just a shade lighter than his brown, wavy hair, which was a lot longer now than the military cut he had first worn after high school. That was when he had joined ROTC, when they both went to college at the University of

Maryland. He remained utterly handsome, despite looking older, more mature.

More appealing, damn him.

"Let's both sit down," he said. "Then you can ask your questions."

Would he answer any? She certainly had a lot—and getting answers to questions was her life. It was her job. And more.

Only recently had she been faced with the most puzzling question she'd ever had: What had really happened to Brody McAndrews, the man she had loved and lost?

They had broken up after college, just before he enlisted in the army. About six months ago, he had reportedly died in a terrorist attack in Afghanistan. It had been a blow, even though they'd broken up long before that.

But when she'd started researching, to find out how he'd died, she had discovered so many anomalies.

Including the biggest one, to her: Why, after all this time, did she care?

Brody pulled a chair out and held on until Sherra sat down. She rearranged her short gray skirt, but not before he got a glimpse of more of her thigh than she was apparently comfortable showing.

Fine with him. The less she turned him on, the better.

But he knew that hint of skin was irrelevant. Despite all common sense, he was turned on just by being in her presence again.

He sat down facing her, carefully putting the knives on the floor beside him.

"Okay." She stared into his eyes. "Tell me what's going on."

Now was the time to begin the spiel of false explanations he had rehearsed in his head for the past few days, ever since he'd learned someone had hacked into the records that had been so carefully doctored to support the cover story he'd created. Not just any records. Federal records, property of the U.S. Department of Defense.

He'd surreptitiously gotten one of the best techie minds in the government working immediately to ID the hacker.

When he had learned it was Sherra Alexander, he'd almost choked his resource for lying. Only, the guy had proven it.

And Brody recognized it couldn't be a coincidence.

"First, tell me what you've been up to, Sherra." He attempted the most innocent look possible as he watched her reaction.

"You've got to be kidding, Brody."

"Not at all. I'm interested."

She stood so suddenly that the chair nearly toppled backward onto the floor. "This isn't a damned get-acquainted date, Brody. You broke into my apartment. You grabbed me. Scared me. And now you want to hold some kind of squirrely flirtatious conversation instead of answering—"

He stood almost as abruptly and approached her. She stood her ground as his chest almost touched hers. Bad idea. Not with her firm, prominent—sexy—bust so close that the proximity got his internal juices simmering once more.

"You work with computers, Sherra," he said through gritted teeth as he glared down into her dark, flashing eyes. "I know that. I also know you've hacked into federal records. If I notified the right people, you'd be arrested for cybercrime or espionage or even worse."

Her stare wavered and she paled a little before squaring her shoulders again. "Why didn't you tell them, then?" she demanded.

He scowled. How much could he divulge without making matters more complicated?

"Is that coffee ready yet?" he asked to momentarily diffuse the situation.

She blinked, then shrugged. "Sit down. I'll pour you a cup."

In a minute, they were squared off across the table once more. It was time. He had to tell her enough to get her to listen—and to heed what he said.

He took a sip of the strong coffee from a large, white mug that matched hers. "If you promise not to divulge anything I say here to anyone, I'll tell you a story, Sherra."

"And if I say I promise, you'll trust me?" She sounded scornful.

"I have to trust you," he said. "You know I'm alive."

Her eyes caught his again. She nodded thoughtfully. "There is that. Tell me."

He didn't need to tell her everything, like the reasons he had done what he'd had to. But he did explain that he'd been surprised, while stationed in Afghanistan as a U.S. Army lieutenant, to meet a private whose name was similar to his—Brody Andrews, instead of McAndrews. They had become friends despite the difference in rank.

Then, one day, they had been in a convoy that was destroyed by an improvised explosive device.

No need to explain to her that although it appeared to be armed by a local group of insurgents, it had actually been set up by someone from the U.S. who was supposed to be on their side. Or that he had anticipated some kind of attack by that someone.

And definitely no need to tell her how angry Brody was that his friend had been blown up instead of him. How guilty he felt.

How he intended to bring down those who'd caused it. Fast, hard and permanently.

"Brody Andrews was killed," Brody said. He opened his mouth to continue, but Sherra interrupted.

"I knew it. The news reported that it was you." She stopped for an instant and he saw her swallow, as if in pain. "I wanted to learn more," she continued. "How it happened. Why it happened." Her eyes met his again. "Whether you suffered."

"I—" he began, but she didn't stop talking.

"But when I looked into it there were so many inconsistencies. ID numbers that didn't match—or were played with—and more. Oh, Brody, I was so relieved to think it wasn't you, but I needed to learn the truth. To find out why your death was reported and why no one else seemed to have caught the discrepancies—or whether I was all wrong after all. I—"

"You kept poking your nose into things that didn't concern you," he said coldly, ignoring the flood of warmth that had passed through him when she'd expressed her relief. It meant nothing—only that she'd been on a computer quest that had started to bear fruit. Not that she cared about him any longer—no more than he cared about her.

That had been over when she'd dumped him around the time they graduated from college. He'd refused to listen to her before that and get out of ROTC. Instead, he'd remained in the program and gone into the army as soon as he graduated.

"You're right," she said sadly. "They didn't concern me. But—"

"But your hacking concerns both of us. There was a reason why things were set up to appear that I was killed instead of Brody Andrews. And now, thanks to you, the wrong people may be aware of the truth. You have to stop, Sherra. Now."

Her expression took on the stubbornness that had once been so familiar to him. But then she relaxed.

"You're right. At least to some extent. I don't have to try to find out whether you really died or not, since I know now that you didn't. I can stop looking into that."

He had to be blunt but couldn't give her all the information that would definitely convince her to listen. "You need to give up your hacking, Sherra. Now. In fact, you should stay off the internet altogether—at least from here, where you're alone. The wrong people are looking for you and can track you."

She laughed, as if he had just told a joke. "But it's my job to use the internet, and I often work from home. I'm not hacking. Not exactly. And I'm not about to give up my internet access just because you say so."

"Yes," he said forcefully. "You are."

"You've got to tell me more. What's really going on, Brody?"

He couldn't divulge anything else critical, not even the important things that had led to his discovery of her hacking.

For one thing, he was currently not Brody Andrews any more than he was his own, presumably dead, self. He was undercover, working for the government contractor that might have been responsible for "his" murder.

"I can't tell you here," he said—true as far as it went. "I came here to convince you to go to a safe house with me. No internet access there, and I can be sure things settle down before either of us returns. If you come with me now, I'll tell you more." Not everything, but maybe this would convince her.

"You're lying, Brody." Once more, Sherra was on her feet, glaring at him. "I don't know what your agenda really is, but I'm not going anywhere with you."

That's what you think. "Okay, then," he said. "Like it

or not, if you won't come with me, I'm staying here with you. That's your only other choice. And you'd better decide right away."

Chapter 2

Once upon a time, Brody staying overnight was part of the fairy tale that was Sherra's life with him.

Of course she had recognized even then that there was always strife in fairy tales. Ogres and wolves, other creatures or monsters that stepped in to make it appear as if there would not be a happily-ever-after.

But in actual fairy tales, happily-ever-after came true. Unlike in real life.

And that was what Sherra lived.

She took a long sip of coffee. Then another. It didn't matter whether she drank a lot of caffeine this evening since she wouldn't sleep well tonight anyway.

But before she even attempted to sleep, she needed to try again to send Brody packing. No matter how much that hurt.

"There's a third choice, Brody," she said as she studied him. "You can just leave."

"Not going to happen," he responded stubbornly.

He sat tall in the chair across from her. His shoulders appeared even broader than she remembered in the black T-shirt he wore.

And those eyes of his—they used to turn her on by a sideways glance. Even more when he stared straight into hers, like he did now.

She forced her mind to change direction. Her gaze, too.

Years ago, when they'd started out as freshmen together at the university, she had hoped they would marry on graduation. By the time their college careers ended, she knew only too well that they'd never be together that way.

Right now, she needed to focus on the hurt she'd felt—and the fact that, despite his wild and scary claims, he had no right to be here.

"Look, why don't you just give me your phone number and email address and other contact information." She spoke brightly, keeping her tone level and remote, as if she conversed with someone she'd met at a bar and intended to walk away from in a few minutes. "I'll stay in touch. Maybe we can get together again soon, grab a dinner or drink." Not true, of course. Once he left, she would put him out of her mind again—or try. "Right now, I want to get to bed."

His eyebrows rose, and she felt herself flush.

"So you need to leave," she continued without acknowledging the eruption of heat that shot through her at the possibility that he purposely misread what she'd said. That he liked the idea of going to bed with her...again.

"And like I said, not without you," he said, as matter-of-factly as if they discussed the temperature predicted for the next day in the D.C. area. "Just because I can't tell you details about some of the dangers you've created doesn't mean they aren't real. For one thing, I'm not about to let you get hurt. So, if you won't come with me, I'm hanging out here till you do."

"Dangers I've created?" Sherra kept her tone soft but let her anger show.

"Let's just say you've activated them. They were pretty mild around here before you started hacking into the wrong websites."

"Then there are right websites to hack into, some that won't activate the dangers you're alleging?" She was proud that she wasn't shouting, but speaking with her teeth gritted surely made it clear he wasn't improving things between them. "What are you talking about, Brody? Maybe if you stopped being so secretive and explained what you mean, I'd listen to what you're saying." Listen, yes. Give up her ability to get onto the internet to do her job—and try to figure out what was really going on—never.

"I can't, Sherra. And the fact I can't should give you a good hint why. But it doesn't matter. You can't get on the computer here, not now. And I'm staying to make sure you keep off it. And to ensure that you remain safe."

Yes, she could guess why he wasn't explaining. Unless he was playing some absurd game—definitely possible, of course, but she'd no idea why. His attitude suggested he had a duty to be quiet. Some kind of official mandate from a government organization, maybe? If so, which branch and why? He'd been in the army. Was he still?

Was his reported death some kind of cover-up, or part of an official operation?

She wanted to know. Had to know. But she was sure that asking more questions would get her nowhere.

She stood. "Do what you want." A tremor of apprehension shot through her. She didn't really know Brody any longer. Was it safe to have him here?

For the most part, she didn't believe he was here to harm her. If so, he could have done it before, when he'd first grabbed her. But who knew?

"I brought my dinner home," she continued. "I don't have enough for you. There's bread in the refrigerator if you want toast but not much else. I'm going to eat in the living room. There's a reality TV show I want to see tonight. You can sleep on the sofa there after I go to bed." She glared back into his gleaming hazel eyes. "That good enough for you?"

"It'll do."

Hanging out on the sofa was, in fact, Brody's best alternative at the moment. Before she'd come home, he had scoped out Sherra's apartment to look for points of vulnerability.

The main door into the rest of the condo and the sliding glass door onto the balcony off the kitchen were both visible from the living room. So was her office door, so he could make sure she didn't sneak in there.

It wasn't as though he would sleep much anyway. He didn't know how soon the enemy would act to learn more about Sherra's computer hacking.

He wasn't especially hungry but would need to keep up his strength. He watched as Sherra retrieved the bag she had left on the hall floor. Putting it on the counter, she pulled out a sandwich and a small container of salad. She tossed him a defiant look as she stomped back down the hall to the office door and returned with the wineglass.

"Have any of that for me?" He didn't smile at the surprise on her face. He'd been all beer and the hard stuff when they'd been in college, but he'd considered wine a drink for women only.

Now, he appreciated a good vintage wine occasionally, even if he preferred a dark, tasty beer.

Without saying anything, she pulled a matching stemmed glass from a cabinet above the counter to the right of the sink. He enjoyed the view as she had to stretch a bit to reach it, pulling her clothes taut against her curvaceous body.

Making his own body react.

He immediately quashed any thought of what it had been like to make love with the smart, gorgeous woman. But it wasn't memories he feared. It was anticipation of starting something up with her again.

Couldn't happen.

"Thanks." He took the glass from her. She opened the refrigerator, removed a bottle of wine, and handed it to him. It was a Napa Valley vintage, one he had heard of but had never tried. He studied the label, poured a little into his glass and sampled it. Sweet, fruity and, yes, too light and feminine, but he'd take what he could get.

A little, anyway. He was already exhausted. He didn't want to do anything to mess up his awareness. Coffee trumped wine.

Sherra carried her dinner into the living room through a doorway off the kitchen. He watched her as he removed a loaf of her company's seven-grain bread from the fridge along with some mayo. After a short hunt, he found a small, round chunk of Gouda cheese. Not his first choice, but he put together a sandwich. He stuck the knives he'd taken from her into the sink. There were more in the drawer anyway, and he no longer thought she was about to stab him. Then he joined her in the living room.

She had decorated it sparingly, a combo of starkly modern with comfortable country furniture along with classic prints on the walls. It felt as multilayered as he had always considered Sherra. Lots of versatile levels to get to know.

He had gotten to know only a few of them despite how long they had been together. The last layers had been unmoving. Impenetrable, yet needy. Impossible for maintaining a relationship.

She'd turned on a reality show, one of those chases through exotic countries.

He'd been to exotic countries. Had had his fill of them, though he knew there was a good chance he'd do it again. Like his dinner and the wine, watching this wasn't his first choice.

But watching Sherra enjoy it was.

She glanced toward him as he took a seat on a fluffy-looking yellow-print chair at the end of the coffee table that paralleled the couch where she sat.

There was plenty of room on that couch, which was of a shade of yellow that went well with the chair. Not surprising. Sherra had always had a sense of style.

People on the TV whispered loudly, plotting their next move. He paid no attention to them. He had plotting of his own to carry out—for instance, keeping vigilant. Watching the windows off to the sides of the TV. Drapes were drawn across them, which was both good and bad. The wrong people wouldn't be able to see in, but neither could he see out to make sure things stayed safe.

At least this was the second floor. It wouldn't be easy for someone to show up either at the windows or on the balcony without being seen in this densely occupied residential neighborhood.

The team on the television dashed off in a car. Time for a commercial.

Sherra, who'd been nibbling on her burger, laid it on a napkin on the low table in front of her and pushed the mute button on the remote. She had turned on lamps on both sides of the couch, and she appeared even more beautiful, and somehow fragile and sad, under the soft light.

"This is so…well, ridiculous, Brody," she said. "If you're going to be here, we should at least talk to one another."

"Fine. What do you want to talk about?" Dumb question. Not that he had ever learned—entirely—to read Sherra's mind, but he'd been able to read looks on her very expressive face.

At the moment, she appeared exasperated. Irritated.

And beautiful and beguiling and sexy...

He forced himself to erase that last from his consciousness. Or at least he tried.

"You know what I'd like to talk about." She sat straighter on the couch.

She'd crossed her long, slender legs before. Her uncurling them now made him remember what it had felt like, years ago, to stroke them....

"Why does the world—or at least a lot of it—think you're dead, Brody?"

That abruptly got his mind back to business. "That's—"

She obviously could tell what he was going to say and continued hurriedly, "Okay, you've already said you can't talk about it. What can you talk about? Do your parents know you're alive? The rest of your family? Did you decide to do this yourself, find a way to flee the battlefield and make it look like you were dead? Because the research I've done shows a lot of anomalies, Brody. That Brody Andrews in your unit was not a lieutenant but a private. He appeared to survive that IED attack that supposedly killed you, but despite some detailed records that almost made sense, there were inconsistencies afterward, not only in ID numbers but also in accounts of what happened. If you wanted it to look like you'd been the one to die—and I don't understand that—it's not really clear, and—"

"At least you're not denying that you hacked into supposedly secure Department of Defense websites," he said drily.

"I wouldn't call it hacking," she said primly, almost making him laugh.

"Of course you wouldn't. What was it—just practicing your skills at internet research?"

"Exactly." She smiled, and the humor and warmth in her gaze caused his blood to pump heatedly inside him as he returned it. And the area where his blood pumped to made him uncomfortable.

"Tell you what," he said. "There are things I'm not going to explain. Things I can't explain. But whether or not you believe it, you're in danger—and not from me." Not if she behaved as he directed, at least. "If you agree to go with me to a safe house tomorrow, I'll at least tell you more about why I can't tell you what you're asking."

She laughed out loud. "That's rich, Brody. And so convoluted that you could shower me with utter garbage and claim you're fulfilling whatever I agree to now. So I won't agree to anything. Oh, look. The show's back on." She leaned forward to grab the remote from the table, and the movement made her breasts strain against her shirt.

That made him all the more uncomfortable.

Holding what was left of his sandwich, he leaned back and started eating again.

He'd known he would be attempting to outsmart smart people in his undercover operation.

But he hadn't anticipated that the smartest of all, and possibly the hardest to deal with, would be the woman he had once loved.

It had been sheer lunacy for Sherra to think she could pretend to act normal with Brody McAndrews sitting near her on one of her own chairs, eating a sandwich he'd made in her kitchen and playing mind games she couldn't even pretend to understand.

Dead Brody McAndrews, who'd been resurrected first on her computer, and now in front of her eyes. And heart. And the rest of her body, which should not pay the least attention to him. Not after all this time—and in these bizarre circumstances.

This was her condo. Her life that he had invaded and now attempted to control and manipulate.

He wouldn't even extend the courtesy of explaining why.

Well, it didn't matter. He was obviously staying the night, though she hadn't really agreed. She would lock her bedroom door—it fortunately had a lock—and stay inside till morning. Then she would go to work as usual.

If he didn't like it, too bad. And if he tried to stop her, she would call 9-1-1 and get his nice, firm ass dragged out of there.

Extending him courtesy because of what they'd shared in the past was one thing. Letting him take over was something else.

On top of it all, she hadn't paid much attention to the reality show she usually enjoyed. It had just ended.

So had her desire to stay in Brody's presence.

Not exactly true, she admitted silently to herself. Desire was the key. The guy, no matter how odd the circumstances, still turned her on.

All the more reason to get away from him. Go to bed. Alone.

She stood and reached for the bag and plastic container that had held her dinner. He rose at the same time, picking up the paper towel he'd used to hold his sandwich.

"I'll take that," she told him.

"No problem." He started carrying it to the kitchen. She could have stayed where she was but decided it might seem a victory to him. Instead, she followed.

"The trash container is there." She pointed to the pull-out part of a lower cabinet.

"Thanks."

She wanted to scream at their polite, distant conversation. This was all wrong. She wanted more from him, now that she knew he really was alive. She wanted to be in his arms, comforted by his hard body against hers, proving he did still exist.

Which was absurd. Especially under these circumstances. She didn't know anything about Brody McAndrews any longer, except that he hadn't died.

But the man he'd become? Obviously secretive. Crazy? She didn't know. But she wanted to.

"How about one more glass of wine before going to… One more glass of wine?" She wasn't going to even use the word *bed* in his presence again. It had seemed to give him the wrong—or right—idea before.

"Fine."

They returned to the living room once she'd rinsed their coffee mugs and poured more wine. Both resumed their former seats.

Sherra decided to try once more for a conversation. Surely, they could talk civilly about things that weren't controversial.

"Can you tell me anything at all about what you've done since leaving college, Brody?" She didn't like how pleading her tone sounded. But she was, in fact, begging him to talk about what he felt comfortable discussing.

"Well…sure. I was a second lieutenant when I entered the service. You knew that." He regarded her earnestly with those gorgeous amber eyes that she remembered so well.

"Yes, I did." That had been the controversy that had split them apart, his joining the military—even though she'd known for years that it would happen.

"Did you serve in the D.C. area for a while? As I recall, you were stationed at Fort Jackson in South Carolina."

"That's right, for basic training. I found a way to hook up with the Army Corps of Engineers. I was there for a few years. Eventually I was sent to Afghanistan." He clearly wasn't going to tell her what he did, and she already knew he had served in that country.

It was where he had reportedly died.

"How about you, Sherra? I know some of what you've done since we last saw each other but not all. You work for CMHealthfoods in their computer department, right?"

"You know more about me than I do about you," she retorted. "And I'm the one with the background in using computers for research."

"You use them too well." Anger glinted in his eyes. Obviously this conversation wasn't as innocuous as she had hoped for.

She'd had enough.

"I'm going to my room now, Brody. See you in the morning—unless you're ready to leave now." She looked at him with as hopeful an expression as she could manage, knowing what the answer would be.

"See you in the morning," he repeated grimly.

Sherra surprised herself. She brought a book to bed with her, not expecting to sleep.

But the next thing she knew, she was awakened by a strange sound from somewhere in her unit.

Brody, of course. Only, it sounded as if something was wrong. Like a body was being pounded somehow. The noise came from the other side of the wall from her bedroom. Her office.

What was he doing in there? Had he been right? Was someone after her?

Had someone broken into her apartment and attacked Brody?

Shakily, she grabbed her phone from where she'd left it

charging on her nightstand. She'd wait to see what was happening before calling for help—maybe.

She had donned a loose T-shirt and sweatpants to sleep in—not that she expected Brody to burst into her room, but she wasn't about to wear anything sexy with him around.

The bedside light remained on from her reading. She pulled on a fluffy, shapeless robe from her closet and tied it around her waist.

She grabbed a flashlight and held it in the opposite hand from where she gripped her phone. She turned it on, then unlocked her bedroom door.

The sound was louder, almost rhythmic. What was going on?

She carefully walked down the hall, past the kitchen and into the living room, then around the corner to her office.

And stopped. The light was on.

Brody was on the floor inside the office. Alone. He wasn't being attacked.

Instead, he was doing pushups. Fast ones. Ones where his knees and chest hit the floor before he straightened his arms again.

Sherra laughed aloud. "Brody, what are you doing?"

He stopped and jumped up. All he wore was a pair of black boxers. His damp body gleamed in the soft light. His expression was grim.

"I was exercising." His tone was almost a growl.

"I figured, but why now, in the middle of the night?"

He didn't answer for a long moment. Instead, he just looked at her, eyes gleaming with heat and longing.

Which stoked something deep inside Sherra, too. She should run out of there. Leave him to his exercise. Stay far away.

Instead, she stood still as he approached. He grabbed her

in his arms, and she felt his warmth and hardness against her. It nearly made her melt.

"This is why, Sherra," he said, and lowered his lips to hers.

Chapter 3

His kiss was forceful and hot and fueled flames within Sherra that had been all but dormant since their last encounter more than six years earlier.

She held on to Brody as if clinging to him now would make up for all the time since they'd last been together. Kissed him back with as much passion, as much need, as she tasted in the hunger of his lips.

His pleasantly musky scent filled her like an opiate she had never again imagined inhaling.

His sweat-slicked body against her was even harder than she remembered. And no wonder, if he spent nights conditioning it as he'd been doing here, instead of sleeping.

His tongue began to perform additional magic, thrusting into her mouth and taunting until she felt her knees weaken. If she wasn't careful, she'd sink to the carpeted floor, drag him with her and start touching him all over. In fact—

His grasp weakened for an instant, and his kiss, too, cooled.

She refused to let him go. Instead, her eyes still closed, she whispered against his mouth, "I don't understand. You said you wanted to exercise—"

At least he still held her close. "I was exercising to prevent this." His voice was raw, ironic, and she finally backed off just enough to look at him.

"But—"

His half-opened eyes smoldered as they regarded hers. "I want you, Sherra. I was exercising to distract myself. To do something other than—"

"Than this?" She pressed herself even tighter against him, her stomach thrusting against his hardness as her hands moved down the muscular planes of his back until she could grasp his taut buttocks.

He groaned. "Not a good idea."

"I agree," she whispered. "Not here. Come into my bedroom." Even as she invited him, her common sense rebuked her. He had been right to do what he felt necessary to prevent what was happening. They had a history, but it was definitely in the past.

They had only conflict in the present.

Conflict, and an attraction that tempted her despite every warning she could toss at herself.

She pulled away long enough to take his hand and start leading him from the living room toward the hallway that led to her bedroom. When he held back she said, "This isn't anything but sex, Brody. It's not changing anything between us. You've got your opinion about what I'm doing, and I still don't buy it. But—"

"But," he repeated. They were in her room now, and once more she was wrapped tightly in his arms, kissing him as sensually as he kissed her.

And then they were on the bed. He stripped off her T-shirt and sweatpants as she maneuvered his boxers down his legs.

She stopped for an instant, drinking in the toned, muscular appearance of his upper body and legs—and his large, hard penis that she wanted to touch. Did touch, grasping it in one hand, feeling its rigid, unyielding heat.

"Brody," she heard herself gasp as he, too, touched and massaged the key to her sex, his fingers hot and teasing and altogether arousing.

He pulled back, looking down as she lay beneath him on the bed, searching her face as if giving her one last chance to tell him to stop.

Instead… "Please," she said.

He thrust inside her. She moaned at the exquisite pleasure as his body kept moving, and she bucked upward at every thrust.

It felt like mere moments before she reached her climax, and she moaned softly even as he, too, closed his eyes and groaned in release.

He stayed perched above her, leaning on those muscular arms as if he was still engaged in pushups. And then he lowered himself. Gently.

His weight pressed her down without stifling her. She didn't move. Didn't want to ruin the moment.

Didn't want to entice him again—not then, at least.

Only then did she realize what she had done. She had made love with Brody McAndrews with the same kind of abandon that had characterized their astounding, unforgettable relationship years ago.

But it wouldn't change anything between them. Couldn't.

There were so many things he hadn't explained while sneaking so suddenly back into her life and trying to control it, and he had made it clear he wouldn't explain them.

For now, she reveled in the feel of him on top of her. How relaxed and sated she felt.

How happy, for the moment, she had been.

But in the morning, when she left for work, she would tell him to go. To leave, notwithstanding this night's activities.

And not to come back.

Brody wanted to shove his fist through the nearest wall—but he hadn't any energy left. Instead, he stayed in bed with Sherra. He pulled her close so her head was on his chest as he breathed fast and irregularly, his body still reacting to their incredible blaze of lovemaking.

It never should have happened.

But making love with Sherra again...

Okay, he didn't regret it. He did regret the inevitable results, though.

She would believe she had some control over the situation. Over him. He doubted she'd be so sneaky as to try to use sex as a lever, but she'd make assumptions. If they made love, there was something between them despite what she'd said about this not changing anything. Something that would allow her to argue for her own way.

That couldn't happen. Not if he wanted to fulfill his mission: get her damned dangerous hacking stopped. And, yes, keep her safe.

For now, though, he drew her even closer. Listened to her breathing become more regular, then deepen as she fell asleep.

Her body was warm. Soft in all the right places. And sexy? Hell, yes. In fact, just thinking about it made his body start to react again.

He didn't try to stop it—but he did concentrate on using senses other than touch to evaluate his surroundings.

He was always aware of everything around him. He had to be.

Though he doubted the enemy would act tonight, he couldn't be certain.

He knew what he would do in the morning. He would talk to Sherra first—and already knew the likely outcome. She might even believe she'd gotten her way, talked him out of whisking her off to a safe house. Somehow talked him into a compromise.

But she'd be wrong, although he'd allow her to believe it was a concession on his part. It would only be temporary and would allow him to fix things in the meantime.

For now, he stayed alert, even as he let himself enjoy the contact with the woman he had once loved and now craved. Again. Maybe always, whether or not he trusted her.

He stroked her hair softly. It still smelled of lemon, as it used to. She murmured in her sleep and moved her face against his chest.

He made himself relax so he could drift off into a light, controlled doze.

It was the only way to keep him from arguing with her. To allow her to get to her job on time.

Sherra didn't like it, but she'd allowed Brody to drive her to work. And now he was coming upstairs to her office.

"So what do you think of the CMHealthfoods headquarters, Jim?" she asked as they rode up to the third floor in the elevator. Fortunately, they were alone.

"Nice enough place." Brody, his eyes behind thick glasses, assessed the ceiling of the car as if he expected someone to smash through it and attack. He hadn't shaved and his posture was…different. His slouch made him appear shorter and heavier somehow. There was even a different jut to his jaw.

He didn't look much like her Brody.

He'd indicated he was off to a job after he left her, but hadn't explained where or what it was. In a button-down shirt and slacks he'd apparently retrieved from his car, he looked more casual than she, compared with the pale blue dress she wore with low-heeled, comfortable shoes. He still managed to be too damned sexy. Or maybe it was the night they had shared that colored her vision, allowed her to see beyond his disguise.

"It's not very secure, though," he continued, "even with the guard downstairs."

Sherra wanted to argue with him, but why bother? The building was in an office park, and she'd always considered it attractive with its curved facade of brown bricks. The cafeteria was on the second floor, and part of the third floor was stepped to create an outdoor eating area for the employees when the weather permitted. Maybe someone could climb the wall and get inside that way, but they'd be pretty obvious since the open parking lot was right out front. Not to mention a couple of matching buildings facing this one.

His hints of danger were getting to her, making her feel uneasy. Was any of it real, or just his way to assert control over her?

She had been uncomfortable, yet not surprised, when Brody had shown the guard his ID—a driver's license with the name Jim Martin and his somewhat doctored photo. A relatively common name. Not Brody Andrews, or his real one. Why?

What was really going on with Brody?

And when would he tell her?

Maybe never. But that was fine. Once he checked out her office and left today, she'd be cautious and assume he was still following her. She still wasn't sure how he had gotten into her unit, but she'd have the locks changed and get the condo association to upgrade the building's security, even if she had to foot a lot of the bill herself—although it should be at least partly a common expense to be shared by all residents.

That should also keep out the people he claimed might be after her. Oh, yes. He was making her feel paranoid—and not just about the slightly devious computer work she had done.

The elevator stopped and the door opened.

Brody edged by her to get out first. He looked up and down the hall, not even attempting to look casual about it.

Once again, she was glad no one was around. She didn't want to have to explain anything else. As it was, she'd had to lie to the building guard, say that "Jim" was an old friend just visiting town and she wanted to show him where she worked. Actually, that wasn't exactly a lie. Just the reasons he was here weren't completely true.

"Which way's your office?" he asked, just as Miles Hodgens, another IT worker like her, came through a nearby door.

"Same place he just exited," she said. "Good morning, Miles."

The tall, geeky guy, whose sleeves were rolled unevenly halfway up his arms, looked first at Brody, then at her. "Hi, Sherra." Miles and she sometimes ate lunch together—when she was eating—but she had discouraged any fraternizing outside the office, saying how awkward it would be. What would really be awkward would be telling this kind guy who definitely wasn't her type that she had no interest in him.

The polite thing to do would be to introduce the two men who stared as if waging a testosterone battle with their eyes. "Miles, this is my old friend…Jim. Jim, Miles and I both work with computers here."

They shook hands.

"Want anything from the cafeteria, Sherra?" Miles asked.
"No, thanks."

Phoebe, the secretary assigned to four people including Miles and Sherra, kept a pot of coffee going all day. That's what helped to keep Sherra going, not the delicious but calorific sweet rolls Miles was partial to.

With a last glance over his shoulder, Miles headed to the stairs beside the elevator.

"Has he worked here long?" Brody asked.

"You're accusing Miles of something?" Pursing her lips, Sherra shook her head. "He's just a nice guy. And, yes, he's worked here even longer than me."

A few other coworkers passed by. Sherra said good-morning but was glad they didn't stop.

She showed Brody through the door from which Miles had exited, into the room where Phoebe's desk sat by the window. The pot containing the coffee Sherra was starting to crave sat on top of a nearby cabinet.

Phoebe wasn't there, though. Maybe she was in the cafeteria, too, or the restroom. That was good. Sherra didn't want to introduce Brody to everyone if she could avoid it.

Once again, Brody seemed to scan their surroundings. "Does that door lock?" He nodded toward the opening they'd just come through.

"I doubt it," she said. "Look, Brody—"

"Jim," he corrected sharply. "Show me your office, and I'll leave."

That should have filled her with relief. Instead, sorrow pulsed through her. Would this in fact be the last time she'd see him? Yes, if she had her way—but it still would hurt.

"Hi, Sherra," chirped a familiar voice. Phoebe, a middle-age single mother who also loved to play mom to the IT geeks she worked for, popped into the room. Her chubby figure was poured into one of the flower-print dresses she loved, and her eternal grin lit her face.

"Good morning." As always, Sherra smiled back, and it reflected in her tone. She liked Phoebe. "Phoebe, I'd like you to meet my old friend Jim."

Phoebe's already wide grin seemed to expand. "Glad to meet you, Jim." She tossed a sly look Sherra's way. Great. Now she'd have to explain the nonrelationship in a way Phoebe would buy—which wouldn't be easy, especially considering what she'd have to ignore from last night.

"I just want to show Jim where I work." After repeating what she'd told the guard downstairs, Sherra escaped through the door on the right that led into her office. She motioned for Brody to follow. He fortunately complied before Phoebe could start interrogating him.

Sherra tried to see her office through Brody's eyes. It was hardly more than a cubicle, and her desk was dominated by her computer. She had her own printer and a small file cabinet to hold paperwork she generated, although most reports were saved nightly on the company's network. She also kept them on memory sticks in case the system crashed—but it never had.

That wasn't what Brody focused on, though. He looked out her window, which overlooked the parking lot. A matching building was fairly close. He checked the windows. "I keep them locked when I'm not here," she informed him. Not that she thought anyone could—or would—climb up to get inside. It was just company policy.

"Fine." He turned, and his amazing amber eyes captured hers. "I'll leave now. Your environment here appears relatively secure, and it looks like there's enough activity around. Just be cautious. Don't go to meet anyone you don't know, and stay near other people. And don't talk about having a visitor last night. I'll be back later to pick you up."

"Brody, I don't—"

He moved away from the window so fast that she didn't anticipate it. Good thing she had closed the door behind them, for suddenly she was in his arms. He lowered his mouth to hers, and his kiss was nearly as hot as any they had shared last night.

"I'll be back later," he repeated.

"You don't need to," she said. "I can get a ride home. Honestly, Brody—"

"You can't take any chances. Whether or not you believe it, you're in danger. So for now, stay aware and stay safe. And most important, do not do anything on the internet, even from here, except whatever research you have to do for your company. It would be better if you didn't get on at all, but at least this corporate system with its company firewall is safer than somewhere on your own. But don't access any sites besides those you're required to get into for your job—and definitely not the government ones you were looking into—or you won't be able to come back here at all, ever, for any reason. Got it?"

"But—"

"Got it?" he repeated.

"All right, but you have to know—"

It didn't matter what she'd been going to say. He turned, and then he was gone.

Back in his car, Brody looked up toward the third floor of the insecurely configured building, wishing he could see and hear through walls, learn exactly what Sherra was up to at this moment. As if he didn't know.

It hadn't just been the protest she'd been about to voice that irritated him. He had seen in her eyes how entrenched in stubbornness she was. He'd be away for a while, and she would undoubtedly use that as an opportunity to convince herself that she'd be able to avoid him later.

That wasn't going to happen.

Would she listen to him, just do her work and not look into who or what she thought he was any longer?

Not hardly. If he hadn't needed to go to his cover job, she wouldn't be here. He had intended to take Sherra to a safe house last night before showing up this morning. That hadn't happened. Now, he would have to set things up today so he could do what he had to.

And then he would have to make sure that she didn't return here, or perform work for this company, until everything was resolved, no matter what he might have allowed her to believe.

He wouldn't have left her if he'd thought anything would happen today. Tonight was another story. Those SOBs he was after, who most likely knew about Sherra and her research by now, would know she'd be surrounded by people today.

Nighttime was different.

But they wouldn't know—yet—that someone was keeping an eye on her.

He couldn't give up his undercover work, not completely. But he had to put it on temporary hold.

When he picked Sherra up tonight, he would have to convince her that, till everything was resolved, he was part of her life. Period.

He hadn't liked revealing his undercover identity either to her or to the people she worked with. But she was smart enough to accept it—although he expected more questions later.

The sex they'd shared last night had been amazing—but it was only a one-time reminder of what they'd had. She would no doubt be too angry with his obvious lies, and the way he would stick close to keep an eye on her, to want more.

But deception was the only way he could stay alive and keep her—and others—safe.

Chapter 4

"How many resumes have we gotten in for the new distribution manager position, Jim?" asked Brody's supervisor at All For Defense, Crandall Forbes. Smelling like cigarette smoke, he leaned over Brody's small parody of a desk in his tiny office, staring at the pages Brody had printed from the computer that was his best friend here. Not that Brody worked on it all the time.

If anyone paid attention, they might think Brody—no, Jim—had a kidney problem since he left his desk so often. Then again, he also drank a lot of coffee. But although he headed for the coffeepot in the office kitchen and the men's room a lot using the slow, slouching gait that he assumed here, his goal was to keep an eye on the pulse of AFD—who was there and what they were doing. And who they communicated with online, on their phones or otherwise.

"About ten," he told Crandall. "Couple of them look good.

I've put them on top." He held the pages up to the human resources director to whom he was ostensibly an assistant.

Hell, it was ostensible to Brody, but it was real to Crandall and others at AFD. He had a perfect background and resume to have landed this job a couple of months ago... thanks to fudging of records by Brody and those to whom he really reported—high-up special ops army officers and Department of Defense civilians. This position was perfect for what he needed to do here: find out everything on everyone and figure out who was involved with the scams, and worse, being run on behalf of AFD.

It helped that his background, before entering the military, consisted of a bachelor's degree in business. Under his own name, of course, not Jim Martin's. But the knowledge he had gained in school was useful now.

In school...where he had loved, and been dumped by, Sherra. But he wasn't about to focus on that now—except to do what he had to so he could get out of here for a day or two without arousing any suspicion. That way, he could keep an eye on her.

He coughed, not hard to do as he inhaled the stale smell of his supervisor. Then he grabbed a tissue from a box he'd placed on his little desk for just this purpose and feigned a good, hearty sneeze into it, even moving the glasses he wore as part of his disguise.

Crandall, an expression of disgust on his narrow, homely face, stepped back. "You getting a cold or the flu?"

Crandall wasn't much older than Brody, no matter how weathered and worried he looked, or how thin he appeared in his dressy white shirt and loose black trousers. Brody had checked him out, as he checked out everyone else he purportedly worked with here at AFD.

"Dunno," Brody said in as nasal a voice as he could create, then coughed again. He had only been in his undercover role for a short time and wasn't about to ask for a day off. He'd look like a shirker, not good for his longevity here. But if he got kicked out for a couple of days to avoid infecting others while recuperating from a nonexistent cold, no one would think anything of it.

"Sounds like." Crandall's tone was disgusted as he stepped farther away in the small office. "Just hand those resumes over to me, then go home. Stay there till you're not contagious, okay?"

"I'm sure I'm not—" Brody broke off what he was saying with another pretend sneeze.

"Yeah, sure you're not. Just get out of here."

"Well, okay." Brody held out the resume copies. Crandall took them gingerly at the edge, between his thumb and narrow forefinger. Brody figured he'd douse his hands with sanitizer as soon as he could. "But I'll be back tomorrow."

"No, take a couple of sick days. I'll clear it." Crandall's broad nose was in the air as he pivoted and left. He appeared to be holding his breath so as not to inhale whatever germs Brody was exhaling.

Brody smiled as he shut down his computer. Mission accomplished—at least this small portion of it. He rose to exit, telling a few of the friendliest coworkers what had just happened, coughing a little around them, too, and assuring them he'd be back in a couple of days.

Then he headed out of AFD, through the long hallways and down the stairs toward the parking lot.

He would definitely be gone only temporarily while he figured out what to do with Sherra. There was too much he needed to do there to stay away long.

All For Defense was a government defense contractor that provided products and services to the military: everything from food and ammo to be shipped from the States to Afghanistan, to contracting with other outside organizations, both U.S. and Afghani, to build schools for local civilians, and to construct buildings on overseas military bases. Or to raze structures from installations being shut down because of U.S. withdrawals.

Brody was investigating it here on U.S. soil now for the thefts and overcharges it conducted here and overseas. The suspicion was that its executives had bribed a lot of people along the way—and even killed to protect their interests.

Brody McAndrews had just started checking out AFD's operations in Afghanistan when the IED went off that killed him. Or at least appeared to kill him, but got his bud Brody Andrews instead.

Once the surviving Brody got substantial proof...well, they'd pay. Big time. And not just in money.

But first things first. He had to protect himself and others who were looking into this. That meant not having a certain beautiful computer expert make everything crash down on them because of her nosy hacking into the highly confidential Defense Information Systems Agency computer records and learning that someone supposedly killed overseas by a contractor under investigation was very much alive. Someone who was now undercover on a very special mission dedicated to eliciting and exposing the truth about who connected to the U.S. military knew of AFD's treachery and allowed them to get away with it—possibly accepting bribes to do so. There'd been some online communication about it, significantly modified once they became aware of the hacker, but the info could still be uncovered if someone dug hard enough—and so could data about who'd already searched for it.

Instead of having Sherra arrested, Brody would be better off ensuring that she kept quiet while this mission continued, or his undercover identity would be put even more at risk.

But her digging so far, even if caught only by the good

guys—which was doubtful—had potential consequences far beyond Brody's own health. Especially for the lovely Sherra. At least Brody had gotten things in line here well enough that he would be able to drag her off to the safe house, kicking and screaming if that was how she wanted to play it.

But she would go with him.

He couldn't help thinking about last night. Having her in his arms again.

Making love with her.

His body started to react. He wished he could take a cold shower right here. Instead, he did the next best thing.

He focused on the danger she had put them all in. Put herself in.

No matter. Despite his anger with what she'd done, he would keep her safe while he got things turned around so he could get back to work—and get his real job finished.

Still seated at her small desk at work, Sherra checked the time on the bottom right corner of her computer screen. It was three o'clock. Time to leave.

She usually worked late, like yesterday. Loved her job.

But if she stayed until the time she usually left, Brody would be there to shepherd her out—and possibly insist that she go with him. To kidnap her, in essence. Even if he claimed it was for her own safety, and not just to keep her from further research he didn't like.

But he was the only one who had compromised her safety. Had broken into her apartment and scared her.

And then seduced her... Well, okay, it had been mutual. They had made delicious love last night. Even better than before. Her body grew warm at the memory. More than warm. Excited. Anticipatory.

Damn. She stood and grabbed her purse from her desk. All that was irrelevant. She quickly shut down her computer after withdrawing the memory stick she always took with her. All of the IT techies here at CMHealthfoods could retrieve anything official that disappeared, but it was the unofficial stuff, her own stuff, that concerned her.

Pasting a smile on her face, she turned the corner and entered Miles's office, which was as compact as hers.

He looked up, an eager smile on his thin, intense face. "You ready to leave now?"

"Yes, please." She'd told him how her friend Jim had driven her there today and intended to pick her up, but made up a story about car trouble and her need to get home to talk to her condo manager about some remodeling of her building that the board had agreed to. All garbage, but Miles was a nice guy. He didn't mind driving her home.

She knew he'd be delighted if she invited him in—which she'd never do. She liked the guy as a friend and coworker but had no intention of getting involved with him. Or anyone.

Especially not Brody. Even after last night.

She would do all she had to in order to eject him from her life once more. She had dealt with that hurt once. She could handle it again now. At least theoretically it should be a lot less painful than before—comparing a one-night stand to a several-year love affair between two young, starry-eyed kids....

"You okay, Sherra?" Miles looked concerned.

She wondered what he might have read, or thought he'd read, in her expression. Sorrow? Pain?

She smiled warmly. "Just thinking about my meeting with the condo manager. Good thing you own your own house. I have to negotiate every darned thing I want to do with my place, but the good thing is that they sometimes have to negotiate with me, too. Right now, they're going to do some exterior work near my balcony so we need to figure out the timing."

If she were really going to meet with the manager, she would also bring up that additional security she had promised herself. In fact, she planned to attend a condo board meeting to propose it. Soon.

Once she got Brody to leave without her.

"Let's go," she told Miles, tugging her purse strap over her shoulder. "I can't tell you how much I appreciate this."

"Anytime," he said.

"You know," Miles said half an hour later as he pulled his small sedan to the curb in front of Sherra's condo building, "I'd be glad to come in and help you talk to your building manager." He turned toward her with a tentative smile on his narrow lips. His pale blue eyes sagged at the corners, so he looked sad even when he was smiling.

He hadn't come the most direct route but had driven out of the way, along one of Bethesda's main retail streets, and suggested that they stop at a major coffee chain for a chat.

Sherra had gently reminded him of the timing of her fictional meeting, and he hadn't made any further detours.

"I appreciate the offer." She gave him a big smile in return. "But I'd better do this myself. I've got a fairly good relationship with our manager, so I'm sure it'll go fine. See you tomorrow." She picked up her purse from the car floor and opened the door. "Thanks again." She exited before Miles could say anything else.

"You're welcome," he called from behind her. "Anytime."

Sherra couldn't help a small, fond grin that he couldn't see as she kept her back to the car. She walked along the concrete path toward the entry to the wide three-story building she called home. At either side were elongated planters filled with colorful but sparse flowers—peonies and other spring bloomers. It was toward the end of the season for them, late in May. The building custodian would soon replace them.

If she'd really been meeting with the condo manager, she'd ask what was next.

Although she heard traffic on the street behind her, Sherra didn't see anyone else around. Not surprising. This was a neighborhood where most residents worked outside their homes. It was even a little early for school kids to be getting back.

Even so, after being assailed in her own unit yesterday—even though it had only been by Brody—she admitted to herself that she felt a little spooked.

And no wonder. Brody had scared her afterward, too, with his talk about the supposed danger in what she'd done—even beyond the risk she'd consciously undertaken by delving into official government records.

She had already taken out her key. She used it to open the condo building's entry door, then made sure to close it behind her—a concession to her promise to herself to stay wary.

The elevators were off to the right, but she instead headed to the open doorway of the mailroom, with its rows of lock boxes for each unit, their facades drab and functional. From the same key ring, she pulled out the key for her box and opened it. Removing a few envelopes and advertising flyers, she skimmed through them, then wadded them into her purse.

She decided to take the steps, as always, to the second floor. The elevator was fast enough, but the small bit of additional exercise always gave her a sense of self-satisfaction. Plus, it saved time since she didn't have to wait.

Even so, she looked up and down after opening the door to the stairway, again in an abundance of caution.

The stairway was quiet. So was the gray-carpeted hall when she opened the door onto her floor.

Why, then, did she feel so nervous? Because Brody had sneaked his way into her unit yesterday? That was a one-time deal. She'd see him long enough later to—

What was that? She had stopped outside the large beige door to her unit that looked like the five others on this floor. Did she hear something inside?

She waited, listening. Heard nothing. Even so, she considered just leaving. What if—

The door burst open. She screamed as two male forms, grappling with each other, spilled into the hallway. One was Brody—still in the shirt, slacks and glasses she had seen him in before. "Hold it, you SOB. Tell me—"

His words were cut short as the other man, on the floor on top of him, aimed a fist at Brody's jaw. He grabbed it before it connected, though—even as the other man kicked wickedly at him. His boot-clad foot collided with Brody's upper thigh.

The assailant was dressed all in black, but his tight shirt hugged muscles that appeared almost as substantial as Brody's. He wore a ski mask over his face. He seemed to be getting the upper hand.

Brody rolled out from beneath the other man as Sherra, trembling, reached into her purse, looking for her phone to call 9-1-1. Instead, her fingers connected with what she had gone out at lunchtime to specifically buy at a chain hardware store near her office: a can of pepper spray. After the nervousness that Brody had generated in her, she'd wanted something with her for some degree of protection.

Something she could even use against Brody, if he made the mistake of sneaking into her unit again.

Before she could pull it out, the attacker turned and leaped to his feet, facing Brody in a crouched position, as if ready to spring. Brody came at him, but the guy grabbed Sherra's left arm, dragging her in front of him like a shield. "You're coming with me, bitch," he growled and started backing down the hall. "We've got a lot to talk about."

Sherra struggled, but his grip was like unbreakable wire and his arm clamped in front of her, around her waist. Brody came at them but the guy moved Sherra between them.

"Let her go, you SOB," Brody spat. He reached behind him and to Sherra's surprise—or not—he pulled out a small gun. He held it the way she saw law enforcement officers aim on TV: two hands, braced and ready. Could she duck enough for him to fire and hit her attacker?

"Shoot it and you'll hit her." The man sounded almost triumphant. But how did he plan to get her out of here?

Sherra didn't want to know. He held her too closely for her to use any self-defense moves she was aware of, like kicking back at his crotch. If he managed to get out of here with her—well, that couldn't happen.

She hadn't hung on to the pepper spray, damn it. But she still clutched her key in her right hand. It might be her only chance. Not quite a nice, pointed kitchen knife, but if she were lucky…

Glancing down, she saw with relief that the guy's sleeve ended at his upper wrist, and his gloves were short. A spot of vulnerability.

She looked briefly into Brody's furious amber eyes, nodded slightly, then used the sharp edge of her apartment key like a knife, reaching underneath to rake it as deeply as she could into the softer skin at the bottom of the man's wrist.

He shrieked in pain or fury or both, but her effort had clearly been effective. Blood squirted over her and the floor. He yanked her to face him, and she used the key again, aiming toward his enraged eyes. Despite the mask, she got the corner of one before he let her go and yanked a door beside him open. The door to the stairway.

Brody pushed by her, aiming the gun. Over his shoulder Sherra saw the man leap over the railing and swing onto a lower part of the stairway. There was blood all over, but she didn't know if it was from the wound she caused or if Brody also had hit the man hard enough to draw blood.

By then, the assailant had pulled a gun, too. There was a loud shot, and a bullet ricocheted around them. Brody shoved her behind the door.

"He's getting away," Sherra protested.

"Stay here." Brody headed back into the stairwell, pulling the door closed behind him.

Sherra was terrified for him. He was armed, but so was the assailant. Would Brody be all right?

Surely she hadn't come to realize that he was alive, only to lose him again while he protected her.

Sitting on the floor, tears running down her face, she reached into her purse, pulled out her phone and called 9-1-1.

Chapter 5

He hadn't caught the bastard. Brody fought to contain his fury as he climbed the steps back to where he had left Sherra.

He'd seen the guy jump into a black SUV like thousands of others on local streets. No license plate. That might make the vehicle obvious if cops were looking for it, but Brody had no doubt that the jerk would put the plate back on whenever he stopped. Or, more likely, stick a stolen plate on instead.

Brody had already appeared in public with Sherra at her workplace, so the fact that Jim Martin knew her shouldn't be a problem—although an armed and angry Jim Martin might be, since his assumed persona was somewhat geekish. Even so, the attacker wasn't likely to have recognized him.

Brody shoved open the door to the hallway where he had left Sherra. There was blood on the wall and floor, including the rug near her door. She wasn't there. His heart wrenched sideways, though he realized she was undoubtedly safe inside her unit. Preferably with the door locked.

But there was always the possibility that the SOB who'd attacked her had an accomplice waiting. Damn it. He should have considered that before hauling ass after the jerk he'd seen.

Brody rapped heavily on the door. He heard a noise on the other side. Good. She wasn't just opening it without knowing who was there. "Sherra, it's me," he called. Was it her? Was she alone?

The door opened, and there she was, brown eyes damp and stricken. He didn't know who initiated it, but in moments she was in his arms. "Oh, Brody, I was so worried he'd hurt you."

He barked out a surprised laugh as he pulled her back into the unit, then shut and locked the door. That was her reaction—when the guy had broken into her apartment to wait for her, then tried to carry her off? Worry for him?

"He got away," Brody told her.

"I'm glad you didn't just shoot him on the street," she said against the front of his shoulder, where she rested her face. "Too many witnesses. Too many questions. But… I did call the cops. They're on their way."

Brody pulled back from her. "Not good." He stared, trying not to let his sudden anger wash over her. "I just want to get you away from here."

Her breathing was heavy as she chewed on her lips. "I guess…well, I'll go with you. For now. But I will come back here. Soon. And to do that, to make sure my neighbors stay safe, I need to let the authorities know what happened here—even if I don't tell them why." She stepped back, and the expression on her pale but lovely face hardened. "Not that I know why. Not really. But you'll tell me if I go with you. Do you promise, Brody?"

"I've told you enough already," he said stiffly.

"Not hardly."

A buzzer sounded. "That's someone wanting to get into the building," Sherra said. "If it's the police, I'll let them in, then we'll talk to them. Both of us, so you can help direct the conversation. But you will tell them something credible, Brody. Otherwise, I'll do it—and you might not like how close to the truth I keep it."

Brody was certainly a good liar. Sherra had to hand it to him. He came up with a story that the cops seemed to buy into, about a guy who had broken into the building apparently to steal from the residents and just happened to break into her unit while Brody, in his Jim Martin persona, was there. His gun had disappeared, probably hidden temporarily in her apartment.

They sat in her living room to talk. How odd—as if she were having a party, with a couple of uniformed cops as guests. She offered them drinks—only water. They took her up on that as they made notes while talking mostly to Brody. Her turn would come, but Brody monopolized them for now. He was creating the story she would need to confirm.

A crime scene team was on the way, presumably to gather fingerprints and blood samples. Would they identify the intruder?

Brody sat close to Sherra on her sofa, pressed gently against her side. She didn't want to feel his physical presence as reassuring, but it was.

Unsurprisingly, the older cop, sitting on Sherra's yellow floral chair, was the one asking questions. The stolid expression on a face lined with wrinkles suggested he'd heard it all before but was doing his duty by listening once more.

"So you were already in this apartment when the door opened?" Officer Arlen said.

"That's right. I thought it was Sherra at first." Sherra hadn't seen an expression this innocent on Brody's face since they were both high school kids and he'd said hello to her grandparents when he picked her up for their first date.

He had strongly hinted to the cops that Sherra and he were more than good friends. That was why he'd happened to be around when the guy entered her unit.

Sherra wasn't about to tell them the truth about their relationship. Their nonrelationship—notwithstanding their lovemaking the night before. But was Brody's approach in her best interests, and not just his?

She glanced over her coffee table toward the chair from the kitchen where the younger cop sat. Officer Evans was female, hair clipped at the nape of her neck, eyes wide and the expression on her attractive, deep-toned face made it clear that she, at least, gave a damn. She seemed to eat up Brody's story, dewy-eyed over the sort of dorky guy—Brody was still in his hunched-over undercover mode, wearing glasses—doing his all to protect his sweetheart. Even attacking the intruder, knocking him to the floor and grabbing the gun he felt in the bad guy's pocket.

That was a safer story for Brody's cover than admitting he had a weapon of his own.

But, his story went, the intruder actually carried two guns. Hence the fact that they shot at each other in the stairwell before the intruder got away.

Then it was Sherra's turn. "I really don't know much except that I was so scared for Jim. He protected me, the way he pounced on that guy, then followed to make sure he left. The gunfire—I was so afraid Jim would be hurt."

"Not enough blood to indicate he shot the guy," Officer Arlen said. "Looks like it was all from the fight in the doorway."

Sherra wondered if any might be Brody's but saw no

wounds on him. His DNA was probably in the system because he was a soldier, but she'd no doubt he would want to hide his identity this way, too, if possible.

Eventually, a crime scene tech came in and took their samples.

"We may have more questions," the male cop said as they got ready to leave.

"Anytime, Officer." Brody sounded sincere. But when he shut the door behind them he looked at Sherra and growled in a low tone, "This was a farce. One that could blow my cover for what I really need to be doing here. We should have left before the cops arrived. Better yet, you shouldn't have called them."

"The entry door from the garage had been jimmied open, you know." She strode back into the living room, and he followed. She didn't sit, though. They were about to have a confrontation, and she wouldn't put herself at a disadvantage. Instead, she picked up the chair from the kitchen and returned it. "The condo manager, maybe residents, too, would have asked a lot of questions. They'd have realized something happened here and sent the cops looking for me if I simply disappeared."

She'd have to actually get in touch with the manager now, as she'd claimed to Miles—and make sure the board soon voted on upgrading the condo's security facilities. Substantially.

Not to mention getting the blood cleaned up.

"They wouldn't have found you." He leaned against the kitchen doorjamb, sounding so confident that she shuddered inside. Did that mean he'd have done something to ensure their failure?

"I'd still have to explain when I came back here," she said softly, hands still on the back of the chair she'd carried. She forced herself to glare defiantly into his angry amber eyes.

"Who said you're coming back?"

She waited a beat, not deigning to answer. Of course she was coming back, if she even went with him now at all. Then she said, "You know, you could tell me what a great job I did backing up your lies to the authorities. How I helped you keep your cover, even though you've hardly told me anything about why you even have a damned cover." She had crossed her arms over her chest, and saw his gaze travel that direction. She was still in the blue dress she had worn to work but wished she'd put on an oversize sweatshirt.

"You did a great job backing up my lies to the authorities," he parroted in a tone that almost sounded amused. Good. Were things between them easing up again? His next words, though, confirmed otherwise. "Now grab a suitcase and put enough clothes in to ensure you won't need anything for a while. If you do, we'll have to buy it."

She stood still, refusing to obey his orders.

"That guy could come back. Bring reinforcements. It's not me they're after, Sherra." No humor in his tone now. In fact, his words, spoken so seriously, sent tremors of fear through her.

She needed more information. A lot more. And she would come back here, she promised herself.

But for now… "What's the climate of where we're going?" she asked. "So I can know what to bring."

Their destination wasn't far in distance. In attitude, it was farther, at least the way Brody had planned it.

With Sherra in the passenger seat, he drove toward it now, along I-95, in his rented SUV. He'd had good reason to assume that the man he had chased from Sherra's condo had played games with his license plate. It was what he, too, had done. This vehicle wasn't easily identifiable by sight, either, since there were so many matching ones on the road.

He had also masked the logo that showed that this belonged to a major car rental company.

Plus, he was being careful, using driving techniques to ensure they weren't being followed. The danger wasn't over. Fortunately, he'd been able to retrieve his military semiautomatic pistol and hide it in the glove compartment.

He occasionally tried to veil road noise with music from a middle-of-the-road radio station but kept it low, trying to soothe Sherra now and then with insipid comments about their drive. He doubted it was working. But total silence wasn't a good idea, either.

As soon as he'd realized he needed to get Sherra to a safe house, he had scoped out possibilities and located a place to rent. It was in Glen Burnie, Maryland, about forty miles from Bethesda, much nearer to the Chesapeake Bay than to Washington, D.C. He had also gotten his Department of Defense contacts to create a couple more identities—a second or third for him, depending on how he looked at it, and a new one for Sherra, too. The lease was under their new names.

He hadn't broken that news to her yet but would have to soon.

In fact— "Okay, spill it, Brody. I'm tired of talking about the weather and traffic and other inconsequential stuff. You're not really distracting me. Tell me where we're going."

He glanced at her. He knew that stubborn expression only too well—her bottom lip stuck out as if enticing him to kiss it back into calmness. Which never happened, or at least it hadn't in the past. He'd never been able to distract her when her dark eyes bored into his that way, as if she could somehow spy his thoughts and extract them.

She looked so damn sexy, even though she'd taken an extra few minutes to change into a pale blue T-shirt and darker jeans. The first shirt she had put on had the CMHealthfoods logo front and center. He enjoyed viewing her bustline but the sign made it even more magnetic, especially to male eyes. He'd sent her back for something more anonymous.

She wasn't looking away or backing down now, but he took his time answering. "I rented a house before I came to find you," he finally admitted. "I told you from the first that I needed to get you to a safe house since your online prying had opened a can of worms that I had to crush to be able to fulfill my mission." He managed to keep the ever-present irritation about that from his voice. "I anticipated potential danger to you, too, though I didn't know some jackass would come to your home and try to kidnap you. Mostly, I just thought I'd get you off the internet for a while to let things cool down so I could finish what I had to."

"But why?" she demanded. "And what exactly is your mission?"

He turned off the interstate onto Route 100. They'd arrive at their destination in about half an hour. If he decided to talk about it now, that would give him time to tell her a bit of what she asked. He needed to inform her of some of it, anyway.

But he would prefer to do it when they were sitting down somewhere, perhaps over a glass of wine. Civilized and calm. Not fleeing in a car from a bad situation. It wouldn't go over well anyway, but sometimes the right atmosphere helped.

There was one thing he could inform her about now, though. It would give her some time to stew about it, get the rage he anticipated out of her system, or at least allow it to cool from the boiling point to a simmer.

The identity thing.

"I promise to tell you about it after we arrive," he told her. "Or at least what I can. National security is involved."

"How convenient." She sounded peeved, and his next

glance revealed her arms crossed over her very attractive bust in an unattractive gesture of anger.

"I'm sure you guessed that part," he shot at her. "Afghanistan, roadside bombs, death, mistaken identity. That just might involve more than a little clerical error."

He saw a movement out of the corner of his eye. Sherra had uncrossed her arms and again stared at him. "Yes, I guessed that. What I haven't guessed yet is why. Why did someone die? I'm glad it wasn't you, but why was he identified as Brody McAndrews instead of Brody Andrews? Why wasn't the mistake immediately fixed? Why—"

"Like I said, I'll tell you what I can." He reached over and turned up the radio dial so music again filled the car's interior.

"Brody!" Sherra all but shouted. "I'm with you because I have to be. But you can't just put me off like this."

Yes, he could. For her safety, and his. But he understood her frustration. In her position, he'd feel the same way. He did feel the same way.

"Like I said, I'll explain what I can later. But for now, I'll tell you about the identities we're going to assume."

"What!" He saw her go rigid behind her seat belt. "Brody, I won't—"

"Yes, you will." He'd turned the radio down once more. Although his tone was softer than hers, it allowed for no dissent. "It's the best way for us both to stay safe."

"But—"

He interrupted again. "Here's the deal. We're going to be a couple who's been married for seven years. That's what we'll look like. Since it'll just be us, we can sleep in separate bedrooms, but our new neighbors can't suspect we're anything but normal. Of course even normal couples have arguments, but to the world it'll look like we're living with them just fine."

"Brody—"

"No, I'm not going to be Brody. Or Jim. I'm Bill Bradshaw, and you're Sally. I'm in construction and will be remodeling a couple of houses in the neighborhood. You're an out-of-work teacher studying to get another degree."

"Then I'll have access to the internet?" They had brought her laptop and smart phone—after he took charge of them—and she sounded hopeful. Was she actually buying into this with no argument?

"No. We'll get you a lot of reading material—regular books and some on e-readers that I'll help you download. You can write on your laptop, too, if you want. But no internet access without my participation and supervision."

"And exactly how long do you think this'll be?" Her voice was calm. Too calm. He anticipated an explosion any minute, but he'd deal with it. She had no choice.

"Unknown right now. I was getting pretty embedded in my undercover identity before, but I may need to take a longer leave of absence than it'll take to get over some fake flu. I'm not sure where you'll be when I go back. For the moment, we need to make sure the original plan isn't blown and can stay in effect despite all the hacking and inopportune questions you've asked online. If not…well, we'll just have to see."

"That's no answer!" She finally exploded. "Brody, I have a life. One that may not be the most exciting in the world, but I'm happy. I'm not giving it up because someone—several someones, maybe—are concerned about the computer research I did when I heard that the man I once loved died."

"You will do it, Sherra. For my sake and yours, and a whole lot more. I mean, you'll do it, Sally. Might as well get used to it."

"I don't—"

"Yes, you do," he countered. "You put us both into this

position with your hacking. Now deal with it. I have to."
Once again, he turned up the music as punctuation—and
to take away her ability to contradict him. He knew he'd
hear more about it later, but for the moment she actually
remained silent.

When he again looked at her, her arms were crossed once
more. Her gaze was straight out the windshield. Her mouth
was a grim line of anger.

That was okay. She didn't have to like it. She just had
to listen.

After a while, he pulled off the main roads, then slipped
along others into wooded areas that were actually quite
scenic.

They were also hard to find.

Eventually, he drove onto a gravel driveway near an unobtrusive single-story house painted an ugly shade of brown.
Its far side was along a creek that emptied into a stream that
eventually met the Chesapeake Bay.

If necessary, Brody would get a boat so they'd have alternate means of transportation to keep them safe.

"We're home, Sally," he said.

Chapter 6

The narrow green pillow on the wooden lawn chair where Sherra sat was amazingly comfortable. The view of the softly flowing creek from the back deck of the house was soothing. The merlot Sherra sipped from a nice, if inexpensive, stemmed glass tasted fruity and exotic.

Her mood was wild. Scared. She wanted to throw something.

She wanted to go back to her real life.

Even so, she leaned back in her seat, feigning calm. "Good choice," she said to Brody, who sat on an identical chair beside her, wearing his glasses. "This house, I mean. It's quite pleasant. I especially like this view." That, at least, was true. The nearby homes were eclectic, of different sizes and vintages, but the one thing they all had in common was the view of the adjoining waterways from their backyards.

Brody, too, sipped wine, looking like the serene, casually dressed lord of the manor. He'd even raised his wineglass in salute a few minutes ago when an apparent neighbor from across the narrow inlet putted his boat away from the dock that matched the one behind this house, heading toward the nearby stream.

"Me, too," he said, his deep voice mellowed even more by the light alcohol.

Yes, there had already been wine here when they arrived. A refrigerator and pantry stocked with food.

When she'd commented on it, Brody admitted he had planned more than just renting this house in advance. He'd had every intention of ensuring that she came there. That they both came there.

That he'd planned to take control of her life—although that was tacit, not part of his admission.

As a result, he had gotten it ready for them both even before appearing in her life again. He'd made assumptions that she would go along with what he told her.

Or that he would find a way to convince her.

As much as she hated that, Sherra wished for a moment that this tableau was real, that she was simply visiting a friend who happened to live in this area. A good friend, perhaps. A friend with benefits, like the lovemaking she had shared with Brody last night.

Had it only been last night? So much had happened since then that it seemed ages ago. And that made her crave him again all the more.

She wouldn't mind staying here overnight. With him. Taking advantage of the sexiness of the man who sat so calmly beside her.

And he did look sexy sitting there. He still wore the same navy T-shirt and jeans he'd worn on the drive here. The way he held the delicate stemmed glass in his large, work-worn hand reminded her of his touch on her body the previous night.

She had a sudden urge to put down her wine and make him take her into his arms. Right here. Right now. That would help to get her mind off reality.

But every part of that scenario was a bad idea.

Instead, she again made herself speak conversationally. "I'm surprised we're out here in the open this way. If we're trying not to be noticed, to stay safe in this safe house, what are we doing?"

The sexy smile on his gorgeous, angular face again made her want to throw herself into his arms. "Have you ever heard of hiding in plain sight?"

"Sure. But why are we doing it?"

"Just looking normal. We're not that obvious in daylight anyway." He stood and moved to the deck's railing. The slope below was relatively gentle, and water lapped at the shoreline about ten feet away. From what Sherra gathered, it must be high tide, since there was no indication that the creek bed encroached farther onto the land. Plus, the wooden dock was only a couple of feet above the water line.

She closed her eyes briefly. Was he avoiding her? Or just finding a way to ignore her question more easily?

Not gonna happen. She joined him at the rail.

"We're here now, Brody. I've done what you asked—and, yes, I know it was at least partly for my own safety." At the thought of the man Brody had fought with at her condo— a man who'd tried to kidnap her—she shuddered for probably the zillionth time and took another deeper sip of wine.

"But don't you think I deserve answers now? I mean real answers, not just hints that just skim the surface of my curiosity because of some unexplained claim of national security."

He turned and looked down at her. His expression was stony, as if to put her off. Again. He had, after all, told her—often—that she'd brought this on herself by nosiness in pursuing what really happened to Brody McAndrews.

She now knew part of it, but not the reasons behind it all.

Why had Brody let the world believe he'd died and someone with a similar name had been the one to survive?

Before he said anything negative, though, she added, "That came out wrong. I do deserve answers. Tell me what's really going on, Brody. Please."

His jaw hardened, as if he was preparing to say something negative. She had to stop him. Impulsively, she thrust her body against his, careful not to cause either glass of wine to fall.

She stood on tiptoe in her soft athletic shoes and placed her mouth on his. Or at least tried to. He was tall enough that she couldn't quite reach without his cooperation.

Good thing was that he did cooperate.

She savored the sweet wine flavor of his lips. He, in turn, swept his free arm around her, drawing her closer yet.

So close that she could feel not only the hardness of his muscular upper body, but another hardness, too, down below. One that took her breath away as her insides heated instantaneously.

She wanted him. Again. Right away.

But as he deepened the kiss, some part of her brain, the sane, rational part, considered what was really going on. Though she'd initiated the closeness, had he taken over, trying to distract her? Whatever the reason, whoever was in charge, it didn't matter.

The sound of a boat's motor interrupted as their across-the-inlet neighbor returned.

"Let's go inside," she whispered against him. "More privacy."

"All right," he said. "But if you're expecting me to cave and tell you everything just so we can really pretend to be

an old married couple tonight, Sally, you've got to understand—I'll tell you what I can, but I'm under an obligation
to keep a lot of what's going on covert. Especially from
someone like you, with no security clearance and, judging
by your online snoopiness, the discretion of a mad parrot."

She stared into his face and saw an unexpected twinkle
in his eye. She remembered the expression so well, from
when they had known each other before.

He might be joking. Or not.

"A mad parrot? And here I thought that, if I really wanted
to spill everything, I could pretend to be a reality TV show
star."

"Or a reporter for a celebrity gossip newspaper."

"An out-of-control smart phone recorder."

Both of them were laughing. The pressure was eased.
They were friends again. More? That remained to be seen.

But Sherra could only smile even more broadly when
Brody—no, Bill—said, "Come on, Sally. Let's go in…and
talk."

They sat at polar ends of the fluffy white couch that must
have cost a mint when new. Now, its seams were a bit frayed.

So was the attitude in the living room.

Brody considered it a fairly nice room, with a picture
window overlooking the stream they'd just been viewing
from the patio.

"Bill" had rented the place furnished. The tall craftsman-
style tables on each side of the sofa could have used refin-
ishing, too. The plain but plentiful side slats holding up the
small square table tops looked worn, as if people had used
the furnishings for more than decoration. The TV was far
from state-of-the-art, low definition, on top of another table
that had seen better days. All the furniture sat on faded area
rugs on the hardwood floor.

Sherra, with her sense of style, obviously noticed the contrast between the apparent upscale decor and the current condition of the furnishings. She said nothing when they first sat down, just placing her wineglass on the table nearest her. Then she asked, "Who did you rent this place from, Brody?"

Since that was a nice, relatively noncontroversial question, Brody responded. "I saw the listing online and contacted the local real estate agent. The property used to belong to a local mechanic but he lost it in a foreclosure and it's now owned by a guy who bought up a bunch of homes to rent out."

"Did the agent tell you that?"

"No, I looked it up on the internet."

Brody loved the sound of her laugh, despite the shake of her head and the ironic grin on her lovely face. "So it's okay for you, a soldier, to go digging online, but not for someone who makes her living at it." She sat back and crossed her arms again over her chest.

Brody wished, for a moment, that he was the light blue shirt she wore. Better yet, he wished their cover identities were closer to reality and he could take the shirt off her, as a real husband might do with his wife.

The fact they'd made love last night was irrelevant. That had been a mistake under these circumstances; perhaps a catharsis after so many years apart, considering what they had once meant to each other. But it was still not something that could be repeated.

With effort, he shoved aside his attraction for her, faced reality. "Not that I needed it to find a house to rent, but I have a security clearance that gives me more leeway online. Any searches I do are part of my job."

"Interesting excuse." Her tone sounded wry. "But I don't buy it. No, your searches are part of your secret identity, your bursting in on my life to change everything." She stood and turned her back on him as she approached the window.

It was getting dark outside. The ceiling light was on, backlighting and highlighting them, and that would make it too easy for anyone passing by to see in.

The fact that the across-the-stream neighbor had taken out his boat before told Brody that others with no business here might also slip up the stream and see them. See Sherra.

He quickly joined her and pulled the rust-colored draperies closed over the window.

She turned to glare at him. "I even have to clear with you when I can enjoy the view of the water?"

"For your safety, yes."

She visibly slumped. Bad idea, perhaps, but he took her into his arms.

She laid her head against his chest. He felt her trembling. He reached down and used his hand to raise her chin just enough to kiss her soft, warm lips.

Oh, yes, bad idea. Especially when he felt his body react, hardening and demanding more.

She obviously felt it, too. She moved even closer, wriggling her hips to encourage him.

He pulled away, and the sudden absence of contact was as brutal as if he'd doused himself with cold water.

She blinked, and her lower lip extended as if she was preparing to bawl him out. Instead, she just shook her head again.

"Okay, Mr. Bradshaw," she said mockingly. "Guess we don't have the best marriage, do we? Well, we both know how relationships can go south."

Brody was used to dealing with almost anything. Dangerous situations. Painful ones. Conversations, even difficult ones, were a piece of cake.

So why did her attitude bother him?

She returned to her seat on the sofa and lifted her wine-glass, taking a long enough drink to nearly finish it. "Okay, time to tell me more. What happened to put us both in this situation? Why does the world, or most of it, think that Brody McAndrews is dead? Who was Brody Andrews, really? And what's the story of your being undercover here, and—"

He didn't mean to, but he laughed. "National security forbids me from answering even one of those questions, let alone all of them, Sally. But in the interest of saving our fragile marriage, I'll tell you what I can. As long as you promise that nothing I say will leave this room."

"Or you'll have to kill me. I get it." She said it lightly, then apparently remembered why they had dashed here in the first place—the man who had broken into her condo and tried to take her. Who might, in fact, have intended to kill her.

She visibly swallowed. He wanted to hold her again. Instead, he took a seat beside her on the couch, so close that he felt her snuggle against his body. He stayed cool, or at least wanted her to think so. He did take her hand and hold it, resting it on her jeans—and her much too tempting thigh.

"It'll be all right, Sherra." At her startled expression since he'd used her real name, he smiled. "Like I said, nothing can leave this room."

"As you know, I was pretty gung-ho when I joined the military. I wanted to follow in the footsteps of my dad and brother."

Sherra didn't move as Brody began to talk, not even to squeeze his hand a little tighter.

His touch felt somewhat comforting, but she could have used more. Especially since she doubted she would like the story he was about to tell. Or that he would tell enough to allow her to understand everything that had happened.

But what he was saying? Oh, yes, she knew how gung-ho he had been. It still hurt to think about it, let alone hear him say it.

She merely nodded as he glanced at her as if to seek her confirmation.

"You also know my background, majoring in business before entering the military."

"Yes, Brody." She kept her voice level. "You don't have to talk about your background. I haven't forgotten a thing."

She didn't look at him now, but instead stared at their clasped hands. A meaningless grip. They no longer had any connection that attached any significance to nearness, to touch. If it made it easier for him to talk to her, fine.

But her listening, as necessary as it was, hurt like Hades.

"Okay," he acknowledged. For the next few minutes, he told her more things she already knew about his first days after induction into the military, how despite his having been in ROTC he required basic combat training, which he had received at Fort Jackson in South Carolina.

"Hey, you know what?" he said before telling her anything of substance. "I need another glass of wine. I brought some fruit, too. Let's get a snack."

"Okay." She shook her head as he preceded her toward the kitchen. The light was dimmer there, but she enjoyed the outline of his tall, hard body.

She didn't like his ducking out when, she hoped, his story was about to get interesting.

But she would give him time to restart it.

And if he didn't, she would give him a big push.

Chapter 7

Brody didn't have to turn around to know Sherra was right behind him.

Without looking at her, he pulled the bottle of aged red wine from where he'd left it on the kitchen counter, on tile more decorative than the patterned beige floor.

Sherra was smart. She was perceptive. If he simply began talking about what it had been like to start his new life as an army lieutenant on the foreign, often hostile, soil of Afghanistan, she would know he was not only holding back from telling her anything of significance, but that he was also stomping down his emotions.

He understood why so many comrades returned to the U.S. with post-traumatic stress disorder.

If they returned at all.

While deciding what and how much to tell her, he needed a break.

Better yet, he needed to do his job. Part of it, at least.

"Be right back," he told Sherra, heading toward the nearest bathroom. She glared as if she knew it was just a ploy.

The john was like the rest of this house. Although it probably started out nice for its time, it needed a lot of work now. At least the toilet, sink and shower all were functional. Brody had checked them out before Bill Bradshaw signed the lease.

Now, in the bathroom with the door closed, he pulled his military-issue phone from his pocket and pressed buttons to connect him to his commanding officer, Captain Michael Cortez.

Mike hadn't initially been his C.O. when everything started to hit the fan in Afghanistan. When Brody learned what he had and started reporting it, he'd still kept his local officer in charge within the Army Corps of Engineers as his apparent C.O., but had officially and covertly been assigned someone out of D.C. who handled certain clandestine operations for the Department of Defense.

Not that Captain Cortez's resume mentioned that little item.

"Hello, Bill," Mike greeted him immediately. It wasn't surprising that he used Brody's current undercover appellation since he'd helped to establish it. "Everything okay in your delightful new digs?" Also unsurprisingly, Mike didn't mention the area where those digs happened to be. Not that there was any reason to think the satellite phone connection was anything but secure, but why take any chances?

"Just fine, Mike. I'll send you a description of our trip here and how great this place really is in a little while." In other words, Brody would send him a report about what had happened to precipitate the trip.

A secure report, over an encrypted internet connection.

"Anything else I need to know?" his C.O. asked.

"I was going to ask you the same thing. I'll start my remodeling project here tomorrow. Soon as I get a sense for timing and difficulty, I'll want to talk to our contact who commissioned the work." Translation: Brody would want to talk to one of Mike's trusted superiors within the Department of Defense, who knew his background and had sanctioned the clandestine operation in which Brody participated.

Mike, and therefore his higher-ups, knew there'd been a security breach by someone hacking internet connections—a huge no-no. But taking official action against Sherra would have blown Brody's cover even faster, and given credence to the fact that there actually was an operation in effect.

"I think we can manage that," Michael said. "Anything you need right now that I can help with?"

"No, but I'll let you know."

"Great. Now, be sure to do a good job, Bill." Michael ended the connection. Brody didn't have to translate that.

He needed to ensure that the hacker he had come after—Sherra—stayed under control. He also had to secure his cover here, along with Sherra's.

Only then could he get back to his real, critical, assignment.

Sherra had returned to the kitchen to wait for Brody to emerge from the bathroom. But she hadn't stayed there for the entire time he was gone.

Now, she sat at the small kitchen table, her latest glass of wine half gone. She had extracted a presliced fruit salad from the fridge and some of it now sat in a bowl in the center of the table. She had set places for both of them—small plates, napkins and forks.

For a moment, she had even felt domestic. But appearances could be deceiving, even to the person who created them.

When Brody came through the door, she looked up,

smiled and waved him to the place opposite her. "This is good fruit, Bill. Have you tried it yet?"

"No, but it looks good." He had appeared wary as he came in, a now-familiar expression. It wasn't one he had used when they had known each other before. He had been open in both what he said and how he looked.

She hadn't always liked what was on his mind, but at least he hadn't tried to hide anything.

She only wished that the suspicion on his face made him look terrible, but it didn't. In fact, it enhanced the maturity of his appearance after their years of separation. He had always been one handsome guy. Now, he looked even better with the additional cragginess and deeper set to his amber eyes.

Once he was seated and helped himself to fruit, Sherra said casually, "I never asked before, but do you have conversations with your private parts, Br—er, Bill?"

His startled expression almost made her laugh. "What are you talking about?"

"I happened to pass by the bathroom while you were there." A lie, of course. It had been her destination, or at least the hallway outside it was. "I heard you talking, and no one else was in there, right?"

He glared. "Were you eavesdropping? I'm sure you know I was on the phone."

She nodded shrewdly. "Yeah, I guessed. Who were you talking to?" When he remained silent, she said, "Gee, Bill, if you want this marriage to last you need to be honest with me. Forthcoming. Tell me everything."

"Even the best relationships allow for some secrets," he growled back.

She was glad he believed that. There was one more secret she was keeping from him. A minor one, yes. But he wouldn't like it.

He relaxed a little and seemed to relent. "I was talking

to someone who helped me get the project I'll be working on while we're here," he said. "Remodeling another house."

"This one could use it," she observed.

"Not while we're living here." He took a bite of cantaloupe and chewed it slowly. She liked to watch his expression as he seemed to savor it.

She still liked to watch him, damn it. Especially now, after believing he was dead—and learning he was very much alive.

She had to take back control of her attitude. She demanded, in a tone that was too harsh, "We're here, Brody. And alone. And yes I know I called you Brody—on purpose. If you rented this place as part of your cover, whatever it's about, I'm sure you've had it checked for bugs and all that. So it's finally time. Tell me what's really going on."

Brody poured more wine from the bottle now on the table between them. Then he helped himself to more fruit. All that gave him a few more seconds to consider what to say next.

Sherra was right. He had prepared everything necessary to allow himself to get into explanations with her—at least externally.

He just preferred not to talk about Afghanistan, what had gone on there. What had precipitated his assignment here.

Because it involved deaths of several people, including his bud Brody Andrews.

It should have been him. Not that he wallowed in guilt. In fact, he was glad to be alive.

But Brody Andrews had deserved to live, too.

And right now, like it or not, Sherra was also involved— immersed up to her lovely brown eyes in garbage that should never have surrounded her. Even though she had brought it on herself…because of him.

She had once been more than a bud, too. Way more. And her current involvement was, indirectly, a result of that.

That meant he couldn't quite obliterate his feeling of self-blame about the danger around her now. But he wouldn't let it stand in the way of fulfilling his mission—and making sure that the peril facing Sherra disappeared without harming her.

Even if he had to continue to annoy her. And to remind himself of his own annoyance.

"Come on, Brody." Sherra's voice from across the table sounded irritated. "I can see your thoughts scrolling all over your face. But until you talk to me I can't interpret them. So, talk to me."

He had been staring at his wineglass, but he looked up at Sherra. He didn't think he was in any mood to laugh, but he found himself chuckling at her words. "Here I thought you could read my moods, even my thoughts."

She popped a grape into her mouth, her eyes never leaving his. "That was years ago, when we were only half strangers, not whole strangers like today."

That shouldn't have bothered him, but he hadn't considered himself a stranger at all to Sherra—not before.

He didn't contradict her, though. Instead, he decided it was, in fact, time to comply.

He poured himself a little more wine. "Okay," he finally said. He placed the filled glass back on the tabletop and settled back on the uncomfortably worn chair.

"Here's what I can tell you." He ignored her frown at his reservation of the right not to reveal all. "You and I—well, we didn't talk much about my military goals, but I'd zeroed in on the Army Corps of Engineers. After I graduated from college and entered the military, I took the corps' BOLC— Basic Officer Leadership Course—and was given stateside assignments after my initial training. Eventually, I was sent to Afghanistan to work on construction projects. The idea was to help build infrastructure and get other development projects started while hiring Afghani people to teach them and to promote stability in the area."

Sherra nodded. "Makes sense. Did you enjoy it?"

"Yes…and no. The thing is, we have to rely on civilian contractors for a lot of what goes on there. We hire U.S. companies with a presence to do a lot of the work and instruction of locals. I…well, when I started, I was a bit naive. I was involved with supervision on behalf of the corps. I expected top performance by everyone involved."

Her dark eyebrows rose. He couldn't quite read her expression. Disbelief in his credulousness, or sympathy? He hoped it was both.

"I take it that you expected too much," she said.

"You could say that. Don't get me wrong. Some contractors were amazing in all they took on and accomplished. But—well, even though there are quite a few good contractors, there's also a lot of contractor corruption. Payoffs to locals not to sabotage projects is sort of understandable. But bribery and vastly overcharging the government, stuff like that is inexcusable."

She smiled. "That's made the news here at home a lot. Apparently it's rampant. Were you really surprised?"

He shrugged one shoulder and snagged some more fruit. He wasn't hungry, but the distraction of eating made this conversation slightly easier. "Not really. I just didn't like it. And then…well, let's just say I found my attention zeroing in on one contractor who seemed to be doing the worst job of all. I went through appropriate channels to report what I observed and suspected." He couldn't go into detail, but some of the appropriate channels had issues.

His tone must have divulged something to Sherra. "What were they doing, Brody? What happened?"

He stayed silent, deciding where to go from there.

But Sherra spoke again. "That was what went wrong, isn't it? Something about that contractor? And before you deny it, please be honest. What you say won't go any further than between us, Brody. I promise."

He wasn't at all startled by her perceptiveness. She was one of the smartest people he had ever met. That had been one of the things that had attracted him to her.

That and her sexiness.

Right now, he had to trust her as much as she had to trust him. Besides, who would she contact with the information he gave her?

"I'll tell you what I suspected," he said. "I found indications that the contractor was paying bribes to get work, and to ensure that those supervising its quality and completeness looked the other way."

"Really? Did someone try to bribe you?"

He shrugged one shoulder. "Not so I could prove anything, but that was definitely my impression. I tried to follow the chain of command and let the right people know my suspicions. But I had no proof, nothing tangible. And local members of the contractor's staff that I talked with—well, they'd been at it for a while, knew how to phrase things so even when I gave chapter and verse of who said what it all just sounded like…maybe that I'd been hinting to receive bribes and was after payback when I got none."

He stood abruptly. Damn. Thinking about this after so much time, after he'd finally gotten the attention of the right powers-that-be…it shouldn't still burn him inside this way.

It probably wouldn't, of course, if that whole damned situation hadn't blown up in his face. Literally.

He headed for the refrigerator as if he craved something besides fruit. Instead, he just wanted to surround himself with cooler air—and to give himself a few more precious seconds before he told Sherra the rest.

And he would tell her the rest. She wouldn't stop pressing him until she heard.

"Did someone accuse you, Brody?" The soft words came not from near the table, but from beside him. Sherra stood next to him—and put her arm around his back as if offering support.

He didn't need it. He grabbed a bottle of water and wrested himself away.

"Not in so many words," he spat out. "But there were enough questions...." And not enough answers.

"Okay," she said, once more invading his personal space. She stood right in front of him, looking up into his face. Her expression was much too understanding. Too kind.

He didn't want her sympathy.

Well, hell, maybe he did.

"I managed to secretly contact one of my most trusted instructors back at BOLC. He put me in touch with someone at the Department of Defense he thought could help me. But that person was in D.C., and I was still in Afghanistan, with no one I could trust."

"Let's change the subject a little," she said as if she knew how much pain this was causing him. But instead of easing it, she threw him onto a topic that could only hurt worse. "Who's Brody Andrews, and how was he involved?"

"Damn!" Brody exploded. "Leave it alone already." He stomped away, evacuating the kitchen and heading for the living room.

But there was no stopping Sherra. He heard her follow him through the hall and stop behind him.

"I know you're angry that I discovered there was a Brody Andrews," she said softly from over his shoulder. "And that he was the one who appeared to survive after—"

"After we were out together at a construction site and the IED exploded." Brody knew he was shouting. With effort, he toned down his voice. "He was a new recruit, just arrived in Afghanistan a few months earlier. We'd run into each other and were both amused by how close our names were. We became buddies. I…I needed someone around there I could trust. I didn't tell him everything, just enough to know I had concerns about how things were being handled. He was a good guy. Understood. We were friends already. He was there for combat, stationed in Kabul, too, till his next mission. I'd had concerns about that job site and its condition, so I was heading there to check it out. He had some free time and went with me. That was one of the matters on which I'd expressed my concerns officially and got nowhere. I hadn't said where I was heading that day. Maybe Brody did. But…we were on the road, almost at the site, when the IED went off."

"And Brody Andrews was killed." Sherra's voice broke, and she put her arms around him, hugging him tightly.

"And Brody McAndrews was killed," he said softly against her hair. How could he notice the fresh lemony scent just then, when everything inside him was shattering all over again? "At first it was the medics who got confused. When we arrived at the hospital I was met by an officer who knew what I'd already been looking into. The incident had been reported, and the undersecretary of defense for government contracts, the department my BOLC instructor had gotten me in touch with, had already been notified. I was told I would recuperate, that I was going undercover, and that for my own safety I was Brody Andrews, since McAndrews had been the target and was presumed dead—and therefore no one would come after him again. I was injured enough that I could genuinely be evacuated. And that was that."

"Oh, Brody. I'm so sorry…" She stood on her toes, arms again around him. She drew his head down to hers.

He couldn't help it. He held her close, smothered her lips with his own, and kissed her as if that embrace was the only thing that could save him.

Maybe it was.

"Oh, Brody," she whispered against him once more, and he allowed himself to get lost as she deepened the kiss.

Chapter 8

Foolish. This was foolish.

Sympathy had driven Sherra closer to Brody. But it was more than sympathy that led her to indulge in this hot, hard kiss.

She pushed even harder against him, reveling in the muscular feel of his body, the moist, alluring taste of his mouth.

He responded. Did he ever. It was as though he had taken the emotions attached to what he had been saying and wrapped them into this increasingly heated embrace.

Was this wise? He was hurting, thanks to her insistence on reminding him of what had happened to his friend. And to himself.

She had wanted to ease his pain by touching him, drawing some of it to herself, but of course that wasn't possible.

Kissing him was another matter.

And if she could help to ease his pain with another sexual encounter, would he take it to mean more than it was?

"Sherra," he whispered against her mouth.

"Bill," she managed to say in return, even as her lips curved in a smile that he licked with his tongue as he pulled away.

"You're right." He looked so rueful, his face this close to her, that she gave a quick laugh, then reached up and drew him back, erasing anything else he might have intended to say by resuming the kiss.

And adding to it by erotically pushing her abdomen against him.

"This house you've rented. Where's the bedroom?" she demanded, then regretted it as he pulled away. Heck, they could do anything they wanted right here, on the living room sofa.

But an old married couple like they were pretending to be…

He grabbed her hand, gave a hugely sexy smile. His eyes radiated heat that further fueled the conflagration raging inside her. If he hadn't been holding her, she might have stumbled. Instead, she managed to stay on her feet and follow him.

Fortunately, the bedroom was nearby. Her initial cursory glance suggested that it, like the rest of the place, could have used refurbishing, but who cared?

They had barely gotten inside before Brody snatched her back into his embrace, kissing her while his hands got busy. In moments, she felt him shove her jeans down her legs, but Brody's lips barely left hers as he bent to undress her. One hand moved beneath her T-shirt, stroking her breasts outside her bra. Then all clothing there, too, disappeared.

"No fair," she whispered, as she tugged off his shirt, then his pants. She'd used those same words all those years ago.

She faced him, staring ravenously at his body, drinking

in his muscular form yet again. His sexiness, his maleness huge and hard and inviting.

She waited no longer before resuming contact. He wasn't shirking, either. His mouth circled a nipple as his hands gripped her buttocks and moved her toward the bed. She felt the mattress behind her legs and let herself fall backward. He followed, joining her on the coverlet.

He pulled away for a moment and reached into a drawer in the nightstand. Then she heard the sound of plastic ripping as he tore open a condom. Apparently he hadn't filled only the kitchen for their stay....

He moved on top of her, and then he was inside her, thick and long and amazing as his movements accelerated, driving her need to a crescendo. She gasped as her orgasm started with a punch and rolled through her.

That was when Brody's cry of pleasure filled the air. He tautened against her, his weight heavy but no burden as he lay on top of her, breathing ragged.

They lay there for several long moments. Minutes? Hours? Not long enough. Brody rolled gently off Sherra.

"You okay, Sally?" he finally panted.

"Oh, Bill, you still rock." She rested her head on his chest.

Sherra must have fallen sound asleep, since the next time she was aware of anything was around daybreak, and Brody was crawling back into bed beside her.

Which bothered her. She was definitely not used to having men in bed with her these days. The fact that she hadn't stirred when Brody left was unnerving. Maybe a little scary.

She might not, while they were here, be in all the danger that Brody had warned her about—and that she had seen when the stranger had invaded her condo unit. Plus, they might be far from her usual haunts with new identities. Despite all that, she should remain alert.

"What time is it?" she asked groggily.

"About six. Go back to sleep." His voice was gentle, but the edge behind it woke her fully.

"What's going on?" She sat up. "Where were you?"

He was still nude, and just enough light slipped between the narrow slats of the window blinds for her to see the broad, sexy outline of his body.

If she hadn't been irritated—and worried—she just might want him again.

Well, hell, she did want him again. But first she wanted answers.

"Bathroom," he responded.

"That was all?"

"You want me to describe exactly what I did there?"

"No," she said through clamped teeth. "But I would like you to tell me who you talked to there."

He laughed shortly. "I thought I made it clear that I don't hold conversations with my private parts."

"But you do talk on the phone while in the bathroom."

"That doesn't mean—"

"That you do it all the time? I know. But I'll bet it's the reason you got up."

He slipped back beside her under the pale blue sheets. His warmth slid toward her body, and she couldn't help smiling—inside. Outside, she maintained her rigid posture as she continued to sit, propped against her pillow, watching him.

"What do you want to bet?" he asked

"I don't—"

"How about another round of great sex?" He moved so his chest was against hers—and his shaft pressed against her belly. "If I'm telling the truth, I get to make love to you. If I'm not, you can make love to me."

She laughed. "I can't lose."

"Me, neither," he said, taking her breast into his mouth.

She moaned in delight—and decided that the rest of the conversation could wait.

Sherra had always been annoyingly smart, Brody thought a while later when he could use his brain again instead of just his body. Or not so annoyingly. Her intelligence was one of the many things he'd loved about her.

But her neediness, and her stubbornness and determination that he should stay out of the military—they'd been things he hadn't loved. In fact, they had been deal-breakers.

But she had been right this time. He'd made a couple of calls when he'd awakened at dawn.

Since she had fallen back to sleep now, he rehashed the conversations in his mind as he lay with his naked body pressed against hers. Good thing he was sated, since he was more than tempted to touch her yet again.

Instead, he just enjoyed the warmth of her skin against his and the sound of her deep, even breathing as he directed his mind to things not at all sexually stimulating: his undercover work and the discussions he'd had—or not had—earlier.

The first was to check in with Captain Michael Cortez. Mike had sounded like his usual cool self, but even so Brody knew him well enough to catch the slight edge in his voice.

"So what's really going on?" Brody had asked.

"I got a call from Ragar. He has a lot of questions that I think you'd better answer directly."

That was John Ragar, assistant to the undersecretary of defense for government contracts, a relatively new department started because of all the bad publicity regarding private defense contractors. Brody had no idea whether things were improving now—although he knew he wasn't the only soldier currently undercover with one of those questionable contractors.

Brody reported directly to Mike, but the person in charge of his undercover investigation was Ragar. When Brody had returned to the States, he'd been visited in the hospital by Kennard Murcia, the undersecretary of defense for government contracts, and the assistant undersecretary, John Ragar, for debriefing. And to be given his new assignment.

To the world, they'd told him, Brody McAndrews was dead. That was safer for him—and it meant he could be useful in finding out what was really going on, including determining who was responsible for the explosion that supposedly killed him. The suspicion was that it was one or more persons within the Corps of Engineers, but they needed evidence to prove it.

That was where the undercover Brody was to come in. Ragar would be his primary contact within the department, and Brody was also assigned to report directly to Captain Michael Cortez. He remained in close contact with both of them.

Brody had learned his lesson well. He hadn't trusted any of them at first—or anyone else. But once he got out of the hospital, part of their recruitment process included familiarizing him with the checks and balances within the department's hierarchy. Everyone underwent intense and ongoing scrutiny, especially because they knew there must be military members and civilians taking bribes and worse.

Those reporting to the undersecretary of defense for government contracts could not be among the bad guys. That was one important reason that department had been established.

Today, as soon as he hung up with Mike, Brody tried contacting Ragar. Because of the highly covert nature of his assignment, Brody had access to one of Ragar's private lines. When he didn't answer, Brody had left a message.

Brody now kept close watch on his phone, though he had

turned the sound off. There were enough protective layers in its electronic remote functioning that he didn't fear anyone would be able to find him, but he hadn't wanted Sherra to know who he was in touch with and why.

She'd clearly guessed when.

"Brody?" Sherra's voice was a soft sigh. He turned to see her head still on the pillow, her black hair contrasting with its white cover, her eyes half open. She looked beautiful.

He leaned over and kissed her gently on the mouth. "That's me, more or less," he reminded her.

She smiled. "I guess it's time to get up." Her gaze scanned his body assessingly. "And I don't mean any double entendres. Not now, at least."

What the heck was she doing? Sherra asked herself for the dozenth time as Brody headed to the bathroom for his shower.

Enjoying a difficult situation, she answered herself. As much as that was possible.

But making love with Brody so much, after all this time—well, it could lead to further complications she didn't need.

Even so, she still hoped to use their lovemaking as a distraction to get him to stop acting so controlling.

At least he hadn't suggested that they shower together this time. They used to do that, back in the old days. But he apparently now needed his private time in the bathroom.

She wondered if he would make any further phone calls.

Meantime, she would take advantage of their brief separation. She had donned the fluffy yellow robe she'd hurriedly thrown into her suitcase. Now she sat at her laptop at the kitchen table. Brody had mentioned before he'd headed for the shower that they'd get on it together later to download reading material for her. She'd just jumped the gun a little, finding it in his suitcase and retrieving it.

She listened for the sound of running water, then plugged the laptop in to ensure it had enough power. She had found her office smart phone, too, but dutifully left it where it was since it had GPS and she didn't know if the person who'd invaded her condo could use its chip to find her.

Then there was her personal smart phone, the extra secret she had hidden from Brody. She kept it wrapped in her underwear and turned off, too. She would cooperate with him but still wanted access to the outside world. Private access.

Her computer was nearly state-of-the-art, but she wouldn't use her potentially traceable electronic card that gave her satellite internet access. Instead, when she turned on her unit, she searched for an unprotected signal from a neighbor's internet service provider.

And found one. She wanted to both hug and scold that neighbor. Maybe, when all this was over, she would find a way to warn the person how easily he could get hacked.

But that wasn't Sherra's goal today. Instead, she quickly set up a new email address on a hugely popular internet site, one where she could remain fairly anonymous. Then she briefly accessed her usual personal account and, using her best hacking skills in case anyone discovered the anomaly, she set it to forward all messages to her new address. Was that enough protection? Probably not, but it was at least an attempt.

She opened her new account. Among the forwarded messages were several from her coworker Miles.

She opened the most recent one. It sounded frantic.

Apparently Jenny, her next-door neighbor in the condo building, the person she was friendliest with there, had been coming home as Sherra left in such a hurry with Brody yesterday. She must have sensed something wrong. When she failed to reach Sherra by phone to make sure everything was all right she had called the office to check on her. She had spoken with Miles, whom she'd met at a party at Sherra's. He'd returned to the office after dropping Sherra off and had been working late.

Now Miles was worried sick. He'd also tried calling Sherra and sending emails, and if she didn't get in contact with him soon he was calling the cops.

Great. If Brody wanted to keep what had happened low-key for now, that was in jeopardy.

The distant sound of running water ended abruptly. What should she do—tell Brody she was disobeying his orders and using her computer on her own?

Hell, yes, under these circumstances.

He emerged from the bathroom a couple of minutes later. He must have headed for the bedroom since she soon heard his hurried footsteps in the hallway as he obviously began looking for her. He burst through the kitchen doorway wearing boxers, a towel still in his hand.

He immediately looked from Sherra to the computer on the table. "What the hell are you doing? Didn't you understand that you're not to be on the computer? Or at least not on the internet? Are you asking for trouble?"

She stood and confronted him. "No, I'm not asking for trouble, but you've sure dumped it on me, Brody. Or Bill. Or whoever you are today. I'm being damned careful to obscure where I am in case anyone is looking—thanks to you and your trouble. But right now, you need to let me contact Miles Hodgens from my office or that trouble just might come from the cops. Tell me how you want me to play this, Brody, or I'll do it myself."

Chapter 9

Brody sat at the table facing Sherra, clenching his fists and glaring. Attacking her verbally wouldn't help—not until he heard her story.

"I knew I had to be careful, Brody...Bill." She stared right back, clearly not cowed by his anger. "I took extra steps to make sure I couldn't be found." She described how she'd used some neighbor's connection and played games to hide who was really looking at her emails.

And what she had learned when she finally read some.

"I really need to contact Miles and assure him I'm okay," she finished. "If I don't, he'll call the cops. Then we'll have not only your bad guys hunting us, but the authorities, too. With all that, someone's liable to succeed. I didn't talk to him when I called in sick at work yesterday, so he may not know I've already contacted someone there."

He had to hand it to her. Under the circumstances, she had taken a good, almost careful approach.

Not that he would tell her so. She had no business getting on the internet at all without giving him the chance to observe what she did and be sure that their new identities and location weren't accidentally revealed. Especially since her former location had been discovered and she'd been attacked.

He realized now that, since efforts had been taken online by government IT experts at the Defense Information Systems Agency to obfuscate his change in identity and assignment, the bad guys had even more reason to go after the initial hacker, Sherra, to extract whatever information she had. For now, he needed to protect her and keep her location secret even more than he needed to keep her off the internet—especially since she took steps to hide. But he wouldn't tell her so.

And maybe what she had done had worked all right.

"Okay," he said. "You can call your work buddy using my phone. It's more secure than yours. He's already met me. Just hint we're having a huge fling, and that's why you slipped away. You're fine, everything's fine, and you'll see him back at the office soon. Tell him about the phone call you made to your boss saying you were ill and wouldn't be in for a few days." He had let Sherra call from her phone yesterday to attempt to save her job. "That actually might be a good thing, since we're not sure when you can go back." If things didn't improve, it could be a long time. "Ask Miles to cover for you as much as possible. Tell him you're worried about your job but you simply couldn't resist." Brody managed a suggestive grin despite the increasingly angry stare he received.

"Is that what this is?" Sherra hissed. "A huge— Never mind. I'd rather tell Miles I'm sick, like I told my boss, Vic… but Jenny contacting him that way makes that impossible.

Even if I keep my job, I'll never live this down to Miles. Poor Miles. He'd thought we—well, forget it."

"He wanted a huge fling with you." Brody couldn't stop himself. She didn't comment but her glare became even angrier. The thought made Brody angry again, too. Hell, was he jealous? Ridiculous.

"Give me your phone," she demanded.

He did so, but when Sherra tried to leave the room with it he stopped her. "I need to hear what you say."

"This should be private. It's a conversation with my friend."

"Who could wind up being your enemy, even inadvertently, if you say the wrong thing and he repeats it to the wrong people."

"I hate all this game playing!" Sherra's dark eyes flashed in fury that suggested she hated him, too.

Which shouldn't matter to him. It was better that way. Getting close to her again physically had been a mistake. It could soften his vigilance—and that couldn't happen, for his sake as well as hers.

"Doesn't matter," he retorted. "Just sit here and call him. And make it short."

She hated having to obey Brody. But remembering the guy he had fought off at her condo—as if he ever left her mind—she recognized validity to Brody's claims of danger and even threats to national security.

She still didn't know all she needed to. The quid pro quo for her cooperation should be for him to explain even more—like all that had happened here in the U.S. after his counterpart Brody Andrews was killed overseas instead of him.

But she didn't ask that. Not now. Not when he was allowing her to call Miles—despite restrictions.

"All right," she said quietly. Brody handed her his phone. She fortunately recalled Miles's phone number and dialed it.

"Hello?" His tenor voice sounded shrill. He obviously didn't recognize the number on his caller ID.

"Miles, it's me." He exclaimed something, but she didn't let him get in a word while she continued. "I'm so sorry I haven't gotten back to you earlier. Jenny was sweet to be concerned about me, but everything's fine. Have you talked to Vic? I called in for some sick leave. I'm not too ill…but I'm not sure when I'll be back."

"Are you with that guy Jim?"

"Well…" She would let him jump to his own conclusions.

"If so, you're making a big mistake, Sherra." His voice was cold and remote, and Sherra wished she could hug her friend, whom she obviously was hurting—even though he had no reason to consider her more than a friend. "He seemed like an ass to me. But don't worry about things around here. I'll cover for you."

"Thanks so much, Miles," she said quietly—but he had already hung up.

If Sherra had yelled at him after her phone call, or even acted irritable, Brody would have shrugged it off and left her alone—or at least stayed out of her way.

Instead, she seemed sad. She didn't say a word but just handed him his phone. Then she continued to sit at the kitchen table, staring at her computer though it was turned off. She clearly didn't want to meet his gaze.

He wanted to take her into his arms, no matter how bad an idea that was. He was about to ask what she was thinking when his phone rang. Her buddy calling back?

Brody glanced at the caller ID. Definitely not Sherra's coworker. "I've got to take this." He pushed the button to talk as he walked out of the room.

"Mr. Bradshaw?" said John Ragar. The assistant under-secretary was using one of his covert lines, but Brody had suspected who it was because of the blocked information—and he'd been expecting the call. The man's cool yet commanding tone, plus his knowledge of Brody's undercover alias, cinched it.

"Yes, this is Bill." Brody kept his own tone friendly yet businesslike. "How are you today, sir?"

That made it clear Brody knew who he was talking to.

"I'd like to set up a meeting this afternoon," Ragar said. "There are some new developments we need to discuss. Are you available at two o'clock closer to D.C.?"

"Name the place," Brody said.

Brody wondered what Ragar's reaction would be when he arrived.

Sherra and he sat at a corner table in the back room of the restaurant in Crystal City, Virginia—near the Pentagon—to which Ragar had directed Brody, in an upscale area that included high-end underground shopping and dining.

Sherra sipped an iced tea. A soft drink sat in front of Brody on the embroidered linen tablecloth. He'd considered a beer or something harder but doubted that would make the best impression on Ragar.

Plus, he needed all his wits about him. He wasn't sure what the assistant undersecretary wanted to talk about, but he doubted he'd find it pretty.

Brody pulled his phone from his pocket and glanced at it. Ragar was late, more than a half hour past the time he'd set to meet. But it was still too soon to try calling him.

Brody glanced at Sherra. She'd apparently been staring but quickly looked over his shoulder, as if some artwork on the wall of the dimly lit room had suddenly captured her attention.

Sherra and he had barely spoken in the car on the drive here. Now, too, the silence between them lengthened. It was definitely not comfortable. He wanted to make her uneasy. Teach her a lesson about failing to listen when he had her best interests in mind.

Instead, he was probably the most edgy about it.

"How's your tea?" he finally asked.

She shrugged and took another sip before meeting his eyes. "So who is this person we'll be talking with?"

"I'll be talking with," Brody reminded her.

She shrugged again, and he wanted to shake her. Maybe do something else to show she needed to follow his rules— or at least to get her attention.

Like kiss those lips that pouted so sexily over the straw.

Instead, Brody just sat back and kept his expression stern. He hadn't wanted to bring her but had figured, during that brief conversation with Ragar, that he had no choice. The Glen Burnie house was probably still safe for now, but she'd been on the computer without his supervision. Despite what she had disclosed to him, there was a possibility she'd visited other websites that could reveal their location. Maybe she even found a way to let her buddy Miles know where she was, though Brody had listened in on that conversation. They might have some kind of undisclosed code between pals.

Or not. Brody believed he would be able to read that in Sherra's reactions.

But what had clinched it was her insistence on coming along. Not that he had any intention of obeying her commands. His were to protect both of them, as well as his assignment. But she had made it clear that, left on her own, she'd disappear after he drove off. Would not wait patiently for his return.

She might even go back to her own familiar environment

and ramp up her security—maybe an okay thing for most people in scary situations, but not her. Not now.

Would her presence inhibit the assistant undersecretary's ability to talk?

Facing the dining room door, Brody realized he was about to find out. John Ragar had just arrived.

"Hello," Sherra said after Brody—not, for now, either Bradshaw or Martin—introduced her to this apparent muckety-muck in the Department of Defense. She put out her hand and he shook it firmly. Like a soldier, she supposed, though he was apparently in upper civilian management rather than the military.

"Hello, Ms. Alexander." He took a seat at the table.

John Ragar was a tall, thin man with a face so long that it seemed to stretch his serious expression—appropriate for a government suit. Unsurprisingly, he actually wore a suit, although he had removed his jacket and placed it over the back of his chair.

A server in a white apron immediately came over and took the man's order—a bourbon, neat. He also ordered a plate of hors d'oeuvres for the table, a sampling of crab cakes, oysters and hot wings.

When the server left, Ragar looked at Brody. Sherra had the sense she'd effectively been tuned out. She'd just have to see about that.

She glanced at Brody. They'd been giving each other the silent treatment ever since she'd insisted on coming along. Fine with her. She wanted to know who Ragar was and what he had to do with Brody's current situation.

They hadn't been quite so silent last night, in bed, but there was no indication in any of Brody's looks that he remembered that.

Their hot bout of sex, their deep physical attraction,

was another thing that had effectively been tuned out, she thought. For the meeting Brody had dressed in a beige cotton shirt and khaki trousers. He was also wearing the blankest expression she'd ever seen on his handsome face.

"As you know, I heard about the attack at Ms. Alexander's place," Ragar said to Brody. "Captain Cortez informed me. I had my staff work out your current cover. Does everything in Glen Burnie appear under control?"

Sherra looked at Brody, expecting him to accuse her of trying to sabotage that wonderful new cover. But he didn't spare a glance her way. "I believe so, sir. Both Sherra and I had to smooth out some kinks in getting time off from our respective jobs—her actual job and my cover for the investigation. We're okay for now at least."

"But we need to get you back there as fast as possible." Ragar's expression looked grim as the server brought his drink. "Your cover is growing flimsier all the time." He glared at Sherra, then back at Brody. "We may have to pull you off your assignment, so we need answers immediately. If you're discovered before we've got all we need, it'll be impossible to get someone else dug in there—and I'm not certain we can protect you. I'm therefore working on getting someone to stay with Ms. Alexander instead of you—a 'friend of the family,' maybe, so you can get back on the job."

Sherra opened her mouth to object but Brody shot her a scowl. "Good idea, if we don't get things handled with our new covers. Just give me the weekend to figure it out." He didn't act subservient this time, but as if he would brook no objection.

That made Sherra happy.

She also knew she'd have to convince him she would be a good girl and go along with his orders before he'd leave her...or she might wind up with some strange "friend of the family" attempting to whip her into shape instead.

"All right," Ragar said. "Just a couple of days, though."

There was another interruption as the server brought over a heaping platter of appetizers.

When they each had taken some food—Sherra scooped only a chicken wing and a crab cake onto her plate—Ragar said, "Now, let me tell you the other reason I wanted to talk to you. You need to know that the family of Brody Andrews is nosing around, asking questions."

Brody paused with a wing nearly to his mouth. He put it down again. Sherra saw a stab of pain in his expression before he resumed his emotionless appearance.

"I'm sure they're concerned because they haven't heard from Brody for a while," this Brody said.

"We handled it well for the circumstances," Ragar said. "As soon as you were confirmed in your initial covert role as Andrews, we contacted his family and told them he was on an important undercover assignment and might not be in touch for some time. They apparently accepted that at first. But now—well, it's been a few weeks. They contacted my staff members who were first in touch and started asking more questions. We've given them good answers that should satisfy them again, at least for a while. But there's always a possibility they'll find a way to locate the living 'Brody Andrews'—you."

"That wouldn't be good." Brody's hard stare at Ragar made it clear he considered that an understatement.

Sherra sensed his renewed, deep pain, the guilt at being the survivor. Her irritation with him and his attitude vanished, replaced by an urge to comfort him. But that would have to come later, when this suit was gone.

"No, it wouldn't," Ragar said. "They indicated they might dig even deeper, hire investigators, whatever. We made it clear they'd better not, that national security is involved, and they seemed to understand. If you're contacted, let us know immediately. Be kind to them, but firm. Hint that you're part of the same operation but that Andrews is deeper undercover—and nothing else. Got that?"

"Yes, sir." Brody's response was hoarse.

Sherra prepared to say something, but he frowned at her.

Ragar caught the silent communication and looked at her. "Do you understand, Ms. Alexander? It's vital that the Andrewses be handled appropriately so they don't ruin our operation. We won't get another chance."

"I do understand," Sherra said. "And this conversation has been very helpful. I didn't completely gather before how the two identities were switched."

She still didn't entirely follow why her Brody had been thrust undercover somewhere here in the U.S., or what he was doing. He still needed to explain that.

But for now—

"I feel sorry for the Andrews family," she said, "but you can count on me not to tell them anything about what's going on."

Especially if she never grasped it fully herself.

Chapter 10

"Interesting situation," Sherra said during the drive back to Glen Burnie. "Too bad I don't understand all of it...yet. You owe me more, Brody."

She watched his neutral stare out the windshield turn into a hardened glare toward the four-lane highway. There wasn't a lot of traffic. It was probably late enough, this early evening, for most commuters to have already traversed the attractively landscaped road. That meant their car was traveling fast.

Faster now that Brody was riled again.

She was glad he didn't aim his glower toward her. It, and his attitude, made her uneasy enough.

But she wasn't flinching.

"What do you mean?" His tone was so cold that it penetrated her heart like an icicle.

"I understand you worked with the Corps of Engineers in Afghanistan supervising some U.S. contractors there. You found that things weren't completely aboveboard, and you started trying to fix that. That led to an explosion and the death of poor Brody Andrews, and it also resulted in your being sent back to the States in some kind of undercover position. So…?"

"So what?" he said. "You've got it, or at least all I can talk about."

She sighed. The conversation with Ragar that day had suggested a lot more to Sherra but hadn't answered anything.

"So here's what I think, with some blanks that still need to be filled in. You discovered that one of the contractors— and I'm going to guess it's All For Defense—was doing something really wrong and you felt compelled to deal with that. Confronting them, exposing them, whatever."

"Why do you mention All For Defense?" Brody snapped.

Sherra looked out the passenger window as she smiled. The sun was going down, but it was still light enough to watch the roadside landscaping roll by.

She hazarded a brief glance at him once she'd pasted a solemn expression back on her face. "Just guessing, but you showed I'm right."

He leaned over the wheel without confirming or denying that she had guessed correctly.

Sherra's research, when she'd started looking into the reported death of Brody McAndrews, had yielded that he helped to supervise military contractors where he was stationed in Afghanistan. There were quite a few contractors. A lot had presences in the D.C. area, of course, for ease of offering their services to the government.

All For Defense was perhaps the largest, involved overseas with projects from building roads and airfields to instructing local civilians how to build infrastructure and buildings.

They'd been restoring and resurfacing the road blown up in the explosion that killed one Brody and injured the other. Data on that situation had initially triggered Sherra's inquiries into what really had happened, since, despite the reports, ID numbers and other information did not point to Brody McAndrews as the decedent.

Sherra leaned back, still thinking. The highway here, from Virginia to Maryland, was well maintained—unlike what she assumed roads were like in Afghanistan except, perhaps, right after work was done on them. Until they were blown up.

All For Defense's connection to what happened was tenuous. The improvements they'd been constructing in that area were destroyed. That didn't reflect well on them. Everyone, even civilians, were supposed to remain vigilant in a war zone and recognize explosive devices, preferably before they went off.

But that wasn't enough to point fingers toward the company as somehow being guilty in what happened. They had been, at worst, negligent.

Yet All For Defense was a name Sherra ran into more than once. She'd seen a lot of others, too. But Brody's reaction had told her she'd scored a hit the first time.

"So what do you do in your undercover work now at All For Defense?" she asked Brody as casually as if she inquired whether he had enjoyed the appetizers they'd eaten.

"Don't go there, Sherra." Brody didn't look at her as he spoke in a tone suggesting a struggle to maintain his temper.

"I'm under orders, like you, to pretend I'm someone else," she said quietly. "To lie about who I am and why I live in that house with you. I'm also supposed to act like the man who was actually killed was the survivor, if his family shows up. Any investigation they're conducting, if at all successful, is likely to reveal to them that there's someone allegedly named Brody Andrews who's still alive, even if he's undercover on some assignment." Her eyes teared up unexpectedly, and she swallowed hard. "I understand what they're going through, Brody. You and I weren't close anymore, but I felt so much pain when I thought the dead man was you. Brody Andrews's family must be full of hope and confusion. They're encouraged to believe he's alive but refusing to contact the people he loves, who love him. I won't tell them what I've learned. I understand national security and all that—but my silence will be more to protect myself… and you. Those poor people, though…"

She couldn't talk anymore, not right now.

"Sherra." Brody's voice was gentle now. "I'm so damned sorry you're involved in this. If I could have kept you out of it, gotten someone else to convince you to stop your damned personal investigation, I would have—"

"My damned personal investigation is who I am, Brody." Sherra was glad he'd said that. It upset her enough to exchange sorrow for anger. "You couldn't have kept me out of it. And since I'm involved, you've got to be honest with me and answer what I ask. And all this discussion about Brody Andrews's family… What about your family, Brody? I knew them when we were together—your parents, your brother. They seemed so nice—especially compared with my messed-up situation. My grandparents wouldn't care if they heard I was dead, but your family must be suffering if they believe you're gone. Don't you have any love for them now? Don't you have any conscience?"

Brody winced. Yes, he loved his family. It had been months since he had spoken with any of them, and he hated that.

But he also knew that telling them the truth now, before

everything was resolved, could wind up resulting in the awful situation they believed to be true: his death.

Worse, it could imperil them, too. He was already angry enough that Sherra was in danger. No one else should be involved.

No one else he cared about.

"No," he responded coolly to Sherra. "I don't have a conscience. Is that what you want to hear?"

"Of course not. But—"

"Then we're good."

He reached the highway exit and flipped on the turn signal. A good thing. This conversation was definitely a distraction to his driving.

Sherra remained silent. He shot a glance in her direction and saw, in the waning light, how pained her expression looked.

At one time, he'd have been glad to learn that she cared enough to mourn his death.

Only, reports of his death had been greatly exaggerated for a reason: to protect him as he continued his campaign for the truth. No one should be looking for nosy Brody McAndrews now—and Private Brody Andrews was information-free and harmless.

But Sherra had figured out the truth.

"Did you think about effects on others when you started this, Brody?" The words were so low that he might not have heard them if they'd still been on the highway, with its road noise.

He slowed for a yellow traffic light but didn't look toward her. He had thought about it—and he'd also been surprised about the intentional cover-up of the ID of the soldier who'd died. He thought it might even be illegal.

But doing things this way had been determined to be for the greater good, and he had to agree.

"Actually," he said, "I did. I thought about the effects of my doing nothing, how many people might be injured or killed because of ongoing poor workmanship. How many others were being robbed by government graft, the bribes being made by AFD, who was accepting them, and—"

"Then it was AFD," Sherra said. "And what you learned over there had repercussions not only with civilians, but also with our government."

"You can draw your own conclusions." He paused, then added, "Part of what soldiers are trained for is to act for the greater good. Protect yourself, sure—but most of all, protect others, especially those who can't protect themselves."

"Very noble," she said. "But Brody, even knowing your reasons, that doesn't eliminate the hurt. I know now that you're alive and that you've made some difficult choices, and at least I have some answers now. Your family…well, I can't equate myself with them. When I learned you were reported as dead, it was a shock. But we were over way before then. Your family must be in real pain."

She was right. He couldn't argue with her.

Saying nothing, he made a turn at yet another traffic light, the last before they started onto the smaller residential streets to their rental home.

Where they would be together again that night, pretending to the world as if they were husband and wife.

They remained silent, and he finally pulled into the driveway, pushed the button to open the automatic garage door and drove inside.

In an abundance of caution, he closed the door again before they exited the car. Sherra was out of the passenger side before he stepped onto the concrete floor of the garage. She didn't look at him as she used the key he gave her and opened the door.

She was clearly upset. Undoubtedly angry with him.

It was better that way. They'd keep their distance tonight. He would be able to make more calls. Stay alert.

Not let his private parts rule his sense for a change.

But he knew that what she had mentioned would continue to bother him.

What did his family think about his reported death?

A while later, they were in the living room watching a reality television show with competing singers. They each sat at an end of the plush but fraying sofa. The dull rust-colored draperies were drawn shut. That meant Sherra couldn't watch lights reflected on the inlet water outside, whether from other homes or the moon or stars. The charm of the place was off-limits at the moment.

Which made perfect sense, since the point of being here was to hide from the rest of the world.

Including Brody's family.

Sherra's, too, of course—what was left of it. Her parents had died in an accident when she was ten years old. Her maternal grandparents had assumed the duty of childrearing—and never let Sherra forget what a burden she was.

These days they usually spoke by phone every couple of weeks. Her grandparents acted cordial, if not caring. Glad she was on her own, relieving them of the martyrdom of their role in her childhood—though they continued to trumpet to the world all they had done for their poor, orphaned granddaughter.

She hadn't really thought much, till now, about how they might handle her current disappearance. She doubted they'd give a damn, if they even noticed.

Their attitude had been one reason it had been so easy to fall for Brody, way back when. He had actually seemed to give a damn about her. For a while. Until he'd joined the military.

"So what's next, Brody?" she finally asked after a contestant finished her shrill rendition of a modern pop song and the show segued into a commercial. "When can I go home?" Her current home, where she had a life, and a career she enjoyed.

He aimed the remote toward the TV and muted it, then looked at her. His amber eyes were as void of expression as if emotion was foreign to him. Sherra knew better—or at least he'd had emotions before.

Maybe that was part of what was wrong now. He might still be one hot guy in bed, might even enjoy that, but when it came to caring about anything but his damned mission he batted zero.

That was a major turn-off…yet it still hurt that he stayed so far away in the same room. Physically and, yes, emotionally.

"I'll do what Ragar wanted—let him find someone to stay with you while I return to my assignment. The sooner I get all the answers I can, the sooner we'll bring down everyone involved with the killings in Afghanistan. Then you won't be in danger anymore. That's when you can go home."

She hated the idea of having a watchdog guard her. But without her around bothering him, Brody would undoubtedly succeed. Yet even if he caught the people he was after, would there be others who'd want revenge on their behalf?

And even if she could go back to her real life, could she deal with having seen Brody again so briefly, then having him exit her life again as if he were as good as dead?

She stood abruptly. "I'm tired. I'm going to bed."

She eased toward him, intending to give him just a goodnight peck on the cheek.

He rose, too, clicking the remote to turn off the TV. "Good idea."

Was that a hint that he'd like to go to bed with her? She

looked into his face as he regarded her, too. A flash of some-thing shone in his amber eyes. Recognition of how close she suddenly was?

Something hotter?

She drew closer. So close she could have thrown her arms around him.

He didn't look away for a long moment. Her insides grew molten.

But he walked away. "Good night, Sherra," he tossed over his shoulder. And he was gone.

Sherra stared after him toward the door to the hallway. Damn the man!

And damn her own stupidity in allowing herself to want him. It was over.

Brody refrained from slamming the bedroom door be-hind him.

It would be a show of emotion at a time when he intended to feel nothing at all.

Damn the woman for goading him about his family. He'd considered them from the first, but felt he had no choice except to deceive them. Not if he wanted to avenge Brody Andrews's death, and also survive.

Not if he wanted to make sure that the devils who'd killed Andrews were dealt with so they couldn't harm other in-nocents.

He'd intended things to go a lot faster. And he certainly hadn't wanted to endanger Sherra—no matter that she'd done that herself.

He crossed to the bed and began removing his clothes, ready for a hot shower to bathe away as many of the day's aggravations as possible.

Stripping his clothes off reminded him of Sherra. The

way she had looked at him in the last moments before he abandoned her in the living room.

He'd had to. No matter how much he wanted to make love with her that night.

As he threw his clothing into his open carry-on bag, he noticed where he had left his smart phone: on the nightstand beside the queen-size bed covered with a worn blue comforter.

He thought of some of the phone numbers programmed into it. His parents'. His brother Sean's.

Sean was in the military, too. Special Forces. He sometimes left on missions where he couldn't report in for a while—but he had always managed to return, then tell their parents all was fine.

Brody would do that, as well. Soon—if he could get back and complete his undercover assignment.

But he wasn't in Special Forces. His family understood him to be in a nearly regular military unit, although the Corps of Engineers was at least a little elite. But it was also transparent to some degree. As a result, for now, his family had to believe he was gone. That was the only way this could work.

Wasn't it?

Crossing the hardwood floor, he approached the table and picked up the small electronic unit. All he needed was to push one button and call Sean. Reassure his brother and tell him what was happening.

Sean would understand. He would also be able to hint to their parents that all was not as it seemed—without breaching national security. Wouldn't he?

Brody slammed the phone back on the table. That was wishful thinking. Even hinting to their parents could make them start asking questions as Sherra had. That could endanger them.

Same thing with Sean, though his brother would undoubtedly be discreet. But this wasn't an ordinary enemy Brody was after. It consisted of people who were supposed to be allies....

He tore off his shorts, threw them on the floor and stomped toward the adjoining bathroom.

He needed that shower. Now. Alone.

But the thought of Sherra in that same house, also alone... He shrugged it off.

She was the cause of his current state of mind.

He had to stay away from her.

Chapter 11

The next morning, Sherra rose early. It wasn't as if she'd slept much that night. Not while knowing Brody was only a few feet away, just down the hall.

He might as well have been on the other side of the globe.

Too bad he wasn't. Maybe then she wouldn't feel like a prisoner. She'd be able to return to her own condo. Her life.

Not entirely, though. She would never forget this interlude with Brody.

She threw back the covers and practically leaped out of bed. This was not what she wanted to think about.

Not again.

It was a new day. What could she accomplish?

The room she'd chosen was small, as much in need of redecorating as the rest of the house, with a light, musty odor despite an overlay of sweet disinfectant. It was so different from her pleasant condo that she could never, even under better circumstances, consider it home despite the lovely water views outside.

It had its own attached bathroom, at least. She showered, dressed, strode into the hall and looked around. The door to Brody's room was still closed, and she saw no sign of him. He must still be sleeping.

Or avoiding her.

It was a Saturday, a good thing. She was not AWOL from her job that day. Somehow she would find a way to return to it Monday, Brody's commands notwithstanding.

She'd have to be careful. She wasn't a fool. Someone had attacked her for a reason—connected with Brody.

Brody. Startled, she gasped as his bedroom door opened.

He strode out, dressed in jeans and another muscle-hugging T-shirt in a dark green that didn't resemble olive drab. And no wonder. He probably wouldn't wear anything like a camo shirt or fatigues here, where he was supposed to be a construction guy with nothing to do with the military.

The way it fit reminded her of the hard body beneath. She didn't want to think about that. Or be reminded about how she had craved being with him last night.

"Good morning," he said as coolly as if he addressed a stranger who'd emerged from a nearby room in a motel.

"Good morning," Sherra repeated, hiding her hurt. "I'm on my way to the kitchen. I'd be glad to fix us something for breakfast, depending on what's there." They'd gone out for fast food the previous day when they'd risen after a night of lovemaking and early morning quarreling.

"There are eggs, pancake mix, cereal—"

"Fine. I'm in the mood for pancakes." She walked briskly past him. If he wanted something else, he could darn well fix it himself.

She located the ingredients and cookware and started on it without looking at him. She knew he stood behind her, could feel his eyes boring into her. Watching her act so damned domestic, as if they were actually the husband and wife team that was their cover.

"Why don't you make coffee?" she said. "I assume you have some." She'd noted an inexpensive-looking coffee-maker on the counter.

"Fine."

A while later they sat across from one another. Sherra could think of nothing to say. Most questions she'd had were now answered—even if she hadn't liked the responses.

"What are we doing today, Bill, dear?" She kept her tone low but sarcastic.

"We can go to the nearby mall if you'd like. Or rent a boat."

"In other words, leave this house so I don't insist on getting on the computer."

His bland expression changed into a slight smile—one that enhanced his hot appearance even more. "You got it."

"Fine. Let's go shopping." From the old days, she knew he would prefer almost anything else, and boating would have been great fun for him.

"Great," he said. "I can't wait."

He owed her this, Brody thought as he accompanied Sherra into the nicest mall in the Glen Burnie area. It was a two-level shopping center, with stores ranging from the anchoring department stores to discount clothing shops. Since it was Saturday, the place was crowded. That would keep him on edge. He'd no reason to think anyone had tracked them there, but he would stay alert.

"Have you ever been here before?" Sherra asked as they walked through an automatic door at one of the center's entrances. The wide aisle that stretched before them was lined with stores.

"No, but I've been looking forward to checking it out."

The look in her dark eyes displayed astonishment before it was replaced by a knowing smile that lit up her gorgeous face. "I'm sure you have, Bill. I know shopping is one of your favorite pastimes."

He didn't grin back, but it was an effort to keep his expression blank. As Sherra knew well from the old days, his method of shopping was to go out knowing exactly what he needed and where to find it, and make the quickest trip possible.

Not so Bill Bradshaw, though. Brody was making up Bill's personality as they went along.

Brody wasn't sure about Sally Bradshaw. In the past, Sherra had enjoyed just looking. She didn't spend money on designer outfits but loved to check out a lot of stores, then try on clothes she'd zeroed in on, before reaching a firm—always correct—decision. At least he'd thought so. Everything had enhanced her perfect body.

Right now, that method wasn't a great idea—being in the open for a long time.

Even so, he stopped beside her in a big-name department store as she studied sale racks. She appeared to be looking for a new shirt and jeans. Good. That fit with their undercover roles better than if she sought business attire in anticipation of a quick return to her job.

"What do you think of these tops, Bill, dear?" She whipped hangers off the rack and waved three shirts—a pink plaid, a yellow one with flowers, and a blue striped one. He could see her wearing any of them in her role as Sally, or even as Sherra.

He also had a vision of her—no, him—unbuttoning them when they were alone together at the house.

"They're fine," he said noncommittally, then glanced toward a salesclerk helping a male customer. No one he recognized, but it still was a good idea to remain alert.

And not think of undressing Sherra.

"Fine." She sounded grumpy. "I'll go try them on with a couple pairs of jeans."

"Fine," he repeated. He watched her stalk off, the tops of several hangers looped over her fingers as she headed toward the dressing rooms. The sway of her hips in the jeans she already wore started him thinking again of hot sex with her—and caused his own slacks to grow smaller.

He observed her until she got through the fitting room door. He then drew closer, his hand at the pocket of the loose denim jacket he'd put on, since he'd stuck his compact weapon there. He listened to make certain he heard nothing, then backed off and surreptitiously watched the women who entered the area. All looked normal.

After a while, he headed toward the nearby men's department. He browsed racks of shirts and pants while watching the door where Sherra would emerge.

His phone rang. He pulled it from his pocket and glanced at it. The caller ID number was obscured, so he knew who it was.

"Hi," he said, "this is Bill."

"Hello, Bill. I wanted to let you know that your cousin Roy is going to visit you tomorrow—Sunday. He'll stay for a few nights," Ragar continued, "so I hope Sally won't mind entertaining him while you go on that fishing trip we talked about. Conditions are perfect and I don't want you to miss it."

Brody got it. Ragar had come through with someone to guard Sherra when the weekend was over. Sherra wouldn't like it, but Brody would deliver no alternate plan—although he would want to meet the bodyguard to make sure the guy appeared competent.

"Great," Brody said. "When will Roy arrive?"

"Tomorrow afternoon. That way you can spend a little time with him before you leave."

And deal with Sherra's expected backlash.

"Sounds good," Brody said. "I'll talk with you tomorrow and we'll discuss my plans for Monday."

"Good." Ragar hung up.

Brody glanced at his watch. Sherra had been in the dressing room long enough. He'd need an unobtrusive way to check on her if she didn't come out soon.

Sherra emerged from the dressing room just then holding only a couple of hangers, one with a shirt and one with jeans. All looked well, and there was no one close to her.

Even so, Brody carefully scanned the area for anomalies. No one appeared suspicious, but sometimes the deadliest attackers looked the most innocent.

He walked toward her as she approached the nearest checkout line. They had been here long enough, although if she wanted to grab a cup of coffee or a snack at the food court that was okay—as long as he remained on alert.

Afterward, they'd return to the house.

Only then would he tell her who they were expecting tomorrow, and why.

Sherra understood why this was happening, but she didn't like it.

It was Sunday afternoon. They sat in the living room of the house. As had become their habit, she was on one end of the fraying couch, with Brody, aka Bill, on the other.

Facing them, in a chair with a poorly upholstered seat from the nearby dining room, was the guy she'd been told to refer to as Roy Bradshaw, Bill's cousin. She had no idea who he really was. He appeared to be in his forties, a little beefy in his sweatshirt—or maybe that was all muscle, since he was supposed to be her bodyguard.

She didn't need a bodyguard. At least she didn't want to need one.

Roy's head was shaved but there was a hint of a dark hairline far back from his forehead. At the moment, he was talking logistics for the next few days with Brody.

She hated the whole situation. How long was she going to have to do penance for her admittedly shady computer research?

As soon as Roy arrived, they'd used a gadget to scan the room, and the entire house, for bugs. Again. Brody had done it several times before. Since all seemed well, they didn't have to act like their cover personas.

Brody and Roy—or whoever he was—were discussing that Brody would stay away for a couple of days but remain in close touch.

Meanwhile, Sherra would be there, in Glen Burnie, away from where she'd been found by whoever attacked her. That should give Brody more leeway to find his target and get answers. Who within that government contractor's company had tried to cover up shoddy workmanship and bribery—and murder—in Afghanistan?

It sounded so easy the way these two macho men discussed it.

It also sounded dangerous for Brody. He was the one who needed a bodyguard, not her.

"So you're okay with all this?" Roy asked. Both men looked at her, waiting for her response.

"Sure," she told them.

That was a lie. She wasn't okay with any of it. But she could at least hope this Roy wasn't nearly as astute as Brody.

She would stay here tomorrow, sure. She'd need to get in touch with her employer again to confirm additional sick time, and she'd make sure Brody was okay with how she handled that.

But once Brody was out of here tomorrow, she would do what she did best: research. On her computer if he left it, and on her own hidden personal smart phone if he didn't. Brody would hate it. But she was determined to help resolve this difficult situation as fast as possible.

Now that she knew for certain that Brody's target was All For Defense, she'd conduct her own form of deep research into the government contractor to help him, whether or not he wanted her assistance.

She would be cautious. She would cover her tracks well so no one would know anyone was hacking, least of all that it was her.

Only after things were fixed and Brody's assignment was completed could she feel comfortable about returning home.

But she would return home. Soon. With or without Brody's approval.

One way or another they were heading for a separation, permanent this time despite the fact they would both be alive.

But her heart withered at the thought that this time she would definitely never see him again.

Sherra had assumed Brody would leave that evening to return to what passed for his life these days—or at least Jim Martin's life.

Instead, he hung around. She let him deal with dinner. Why should she cook when she disliked everything going on around her—and had no choice about being here?

He sent Roy out for chicken dinners from a fast food joint not far away.

That left her alone with Brody for a little while—for the last time?

She didn't want to think about that, but she thought about nothing else. As a result, she went onto the wooden deck in back and stared over the water.

She knew exactly when Brody joined her. She didn't need to hear his footsteps resonate on the wood. She felt him.

She shivered slightly. Why didn't he just leave her alone? He was leaving her anyway, tomorrow.

"Are you okay with all this?"

She turned to stare. "You're joking. I'm not okay with any of it."

His brilliant amber eyes bored into her for a moment as if he wanted to use them to drill sense into her brain. But then he shook his head slowly.

"Me, neither. Not really. I didn't start this. But I sure as hell can't give up till it's resolved and whoever's behind it is stopped."

His expression looked unguarded, full of anguish and anger.

Sherra couldn't help it. She took a few steps to close the gap between them. She reached toward him, taking his warm, angular face in her hands, feeling the evening shadow graze her palms as she drew him closer.

And kissed him.

Chapter 12

Brody didn't want to feel better. He wanted to feel the anger at himself that Sherra should be pouring all over him.

Instead, he let himself savor the touch of her lips on his, the way she drew him down to deepen the kiss.

The stroke of her tongue seeking passage into his mouth, which he opened for her.

"Brody," she whispered against him.

His brain reacted finally. "Let's go inside."

He used his body to back her through the doorway and into the kitchen. He closed the sliding glass door and the drapes with one hand as his other arm wrapped around Sherra, drawing her close, so close that his body tightened and reacted all over.

Her hands were on his back, moving downward to cup his buttocks outside his pants. He moved away just enough to throw an arm around her shoulder. "My bedroom's closest," he announced hoarsely.

In moments that felt like eons, they were inside. He shut the door, glad the nearest shopping area was a distance from this waterfront residential area; Roy wouldn't be back for a while.

Sherra's thoughts must also have been on their lunacy and how fast they'd have to act to avoid getting caught. "It'll have to be a quickie," she breathed against him, and he felt her smiling even as she kissed him deeply once more.

They threw themselves onto his bed. He stripped her fast, reveling in the pleasure as she unbuttoned his shirt and pulled off his clothes, too. He looked down at her beautiful body and watched his hands cup her breasts before moving downward.

She gasped as his mouth sucked in one nipple, then the other, but kept her fingers busy, stroking him.

This was foolish.

He protected them both by removing a condom from the drawer of his beside table. She grabbed it and appeared to enjoy teasing him by putting it on him slowly.

Then, at last, he was inside her. The sensation was intense. Incredible. Wonderful.

Perhaps even more so because he knew, on some level, that it had to be the last time. Maybe forever.

Hearing her gasp and moan sent him over the edge to his fulfillment. He held her all the tighter as he groaned her name.

He didn't want to let her go, though it was over. Maybe because it was over.

But sanity won out. "Let's get dressed quick." He looked down at her soft, hazy, beautiful face. "We won't be alone much longer."

That night, Sherra barely slept. Brody was down the hall—most likely also remembering their lovemaking.

But also down the hall was the man known as Roy Bradshaw, her supposed handler.

Shortly after six the next morning, she hopped out of bed, showered, threw on a shirt and jeans, then hurried out of her room.

The two men were already in the kitchen, at the small table in its center eating cereal and talking in low voices she was not meant to overhear.

"You're up already," she said as cheerfully as she could. "And you've made coffee. Great." She hurried to the counter and poured a cup.

"Glad you're awake." Brody stood and approached. "I'm about to leave."

He wore a button-down shirt and dressy slacks. His usually angular features were a bit less sharp this morning, and Sherra figured she had been correct in her belief that he wouldn't sleep any better than she did. For the first time in days, he wore glasses.

"Fine. Have a good day. Week. Whatever." She kept her tone offhand, not suggesting the conflicting emotions ricocheting inside her.

"I'll be in touch." His voice contained no more emotion than hers. But the amber glow in his eyes had dulled into something resembling pain.

Was she imagining that? Illogically reading her own pain into his expression?

"I'll look forward to it," she said lightly. She grew more serious. "Be careful, Brody. I may not understand all you're doing or why, but I know it's dangerous. Stay safe."

And come back to me, she wanted to say but didn't. She wouldn't be here for him to come back to. And although he was well aware of where her condo was, and her job, too, he'd undoubtedly wind up too angry to just drop back into her life on any friendly basis.

She wouldn't allow him back in on any other basis.

He leaned toward her. For a moment, she thought he was about to kiss her, and she closed her eyes in eager anticipation.

Instead, he whispered into her ear, "Don't do anything foolish, Sherra. Listen to Roy. He's here to help you and has your best interests in mind. And despite what I'm sure you're thinking, you can't get back onto the computer when I'm not here. Got that?"

She stepped back and glared up at him, knowing the sudden fury that shot through her like flames from an arson fire must be obvious from her expression. "I hear you," she spat.

That didn't mean she would obey.

"In case you've got anything else in mind," Brody said softly, "just try to find your laptop. And your phone."

"Damn you, Brody!"

"See ya." He waved at Roy and left the room.

Sherra wasn't stupid. But she was determined.

She might not have her laptop to play with, but she did have that extra smart phone she had forgotten—not—to tell Brody about.

"So what would you like to talk about, cousin-in-law, dear?" she asked Roy sarcastically when they were alone. "More breakfast? Coffee? What'll it take for you to leave me alone if I hang out in my bedroom? Better yet, what'll it take to get you to leave altogether?"

Her beefy ostensible bodyguard gave a smile that sent shivers up her body. He was supposed to protect her? He was probably also supposed to make sure she obeyed Brody's orders. Brody must trust him. Then why did he give her the willies just by the way he looked at her?

Maybe it was the way he also scanned her body with his eyes before stopping his gaze once more on her face.

"I'm not going anywhere." His slow drawl did nothing to alleviate her discomfort. "I'm here to take care of you."

She heard the double entendre and rose. "Well, I don't have to take care of you. I'll be in my room if anything exciting happens."

She almost kicked herself as she hurried down the hall, a cup of coffee shaking in her hand. The last thing she wanted was for anything exciting to happen, especially while trapped here with Roy the Repulsive.

She felt a little better in her room with the door closed firmly behind her. She wished it had a lock, but the best she could do was to move its only chair against the door, one with an ornate but scuffed wooden back that must have been lovely when it was new.

She crossed the room to where her small suitcase lay on the floor. She stooped and looked around—as if Roy could see her through the closed door. Not likely. Nor was there any indication of security cameras or any other way Brody or anyone else could keep an eye on her movements inside this house. She was being foolish.

Not surprising, with everything that had happened to her in the past few days. Well, she was going to take back control, starting in this small way.

Only then did she remove the smart phone from the wad of underwear where she had hidden it, inside her suitcase.

She smiled as she cradled it in her hand but didn't turn it on yet. Instead, she also pulled out the cord to charge it and plugged it in, just in case.

When she'd started working at CMHealthfoods a couple of years ago, they supplied her with a business phone with its own number that she could use for personal matters, too. That was the one she always carried with her—until Brody had usurped it.

But she hadn't given up the personal phone number she'd

had before. Although she hadn't upgraded the smart phone that now lay on the bedside table, the fact that it wasn't the latest technology didn't make it unusable.

Unsurprisingly, Brody had taken her laptop and business phone. This house had a landline—Brody had confirmed that, and she had seen a couple of phones on tables—so she wasn't completely cut off from communicating with the outside world. Nor would she have to rely on good old Roy to make calls on her behalf on his cell phone.

But her ability to call anyone on the landline would be limited, since Roy would know about it. Nor would any calls be private—not with Roy listening in.

Little did Brody know that she had other resources. She could make calls from her own smart phone.

And use the internet.

She needed to be careful, though. She wouldn't research anything to put her on the radar of whoever had come after her before. But she didn't need to do that again anyway. It had resulted from her trying to find out what had really happened to Brody McAndrews.

Nor would she do anything that smacked of doing work for CMHealthfoods, in case someone monitored that, too, to try to find her.

But her life revolved around computer research. She was determined to do end runs around what Brody himself was looking into—government contracts for work in Afghanistan, and particularly deals entered into with All For Defense.

She wouldn't see Brody again soon but knew how involved he was in finding answers. His way would undoubtedly be most effective. But she could do some peeking her way, too, in case there'd been anything in the news about AFD or otherwise that might help determine who was behind the bombing.

It would give her an excuse to call him—on the house phone. She wouldn't tell him she was disobeying and doing online research, but would just give him some "suggestions" that came to her while twiddling her thumbs here.

Even if Brody wound up permanently out of her life sooner that way, she would potentially be able to resume that life sooner, too.

She sat on the bed and held her phone, letting it continue to charge. She connected to the internet and looked up All For Defense on her favorite search engine.

Interesting outfit, from what she'd seen before and confirmed now. It was mostly into constructing and dismantling buildings—anywhere in the world. Its largest client was the U.S. government.

The company earned millions of dollars of taxpayer money every year. Supposedly, it bid against other contractors for most of its work. And usually won.

Nothing in what she found suggested corruption of any kind—but what if those bids were rigged?

She dug a little deeper....

And was startled by a knock on the door.

"Yes?" She quickly unplugged the phone and hid the cord and handset in the top drawer of the nightstand. She'd stow it more carefully later, but Roy might push open the door at any second, notwithstanding the chair in the way.

"Hey, Sally. Your hubby is on the house phone. He needs to talk to you right away."

Sherra stood, pulled the chair away and opened the door. Her heart pounded unevenly, and not just because she'd been startled by the knock. "Is he okay?"

"Sounds like, but he wants to ask you a question."

"Okay." Sherra maneuvered past Roy and hurried to the living room, where a phone lay on a shelf near the TV. She picked up the receiver. "Hello?"

"Hi, Sally," said Brody's deep, calm voice. He sounded fine, but he could be a good actor. "This is Jim Martin calling."

"Hi, Jim," she said back. "Everything okay?"

"Yes, but—" His voice grew lower and Sherra strained to hear him. "This line should be secure," he'd said. "I need your help, Sally, using the skills I know you're damned good at. I need advice about hacking into some websites, and most especially email."

Brody hated to call Sherra for that kind of help but had no choice. He'd reached an impasse.

At the moment, he sat at his desk at AFD, staring with disgust at the piles of paper that had grown while he was gone. Wasn't this the electronic era? And it didn't contain stuff he really needed to work on.

He had returned to AFD, emitting a few coughs and sniffles to again validate the reason he'd been away for a few days—a supposed cold. As always, he had to remember his glasses, altered posture and everything else that constituted his disguise here, not that any AFD staffer he'd met in Afghanistan ever showed up.

His supervisor in Human Resources, Crandall Forbes, had sniffed, too—mostly out of dislike at having someone around who might be contagious. At least he kept his distance after their initial greeting. That was fine with Brody, since he still reviled the strong scent of cigarettes.

Using his pseudo identity here at AFD as Jim Martin, Brody made some calls after taking a quick swing through the inevitable emailed resumes. They didn't contain the information he was really after.

But after trying once more to check a whole other kind of email—something he had attempted frequently, from different angles, since starting in his undercover position here—he was totally frustrated. The latest step-by-step instructions he had received from an authorized Defense Information Systems Agency computer nerd with the highest security clearances hadn't worked any better than other suggested methods he'd used before.

Maybe he should have run this question by Sherra previously, but it was something he would rather not have gotten her involved with.

But that was before, when he'd had hope this new way would work. This was now. He had reached a whole new level of frustration. Maybe, considering the passage of time and the increase of tension thanks to Sherra's involvement, it was becoming desperation.

"I can't go into a lot of detail," he said softly to Sherra over his own smart phone. He had once again made certain there were no bugs planted in his office or any other way of his personal conversations being hijacked. Even so, he continued to use their aliases. But what he was about to discuss with her had better not be heard by anyone else. "The email system here is very secure, and I need access to some accounts that aren't my own. I tried things that others in my own organization suggested but nothing has worked. I suspect, though, that you'll—"

"Have ideas about how to hack into a highly secure email system?" He enjoyed the amazed laughter in the tone of her voice.

He pictured her, lovely and casual and altogether sexy, stretched out on the living room couch as they talked. He smiled back at the phone until he realized what he was doing and grew serious again. "Exactly."

He remained determined to get this job completed as quickly as possible. He hadn't succeeded before, and now, with Sherra in the picture, he had even more incentive to succeed fast.

He couldn't keep her at the safe house in Maryland, under guard, forever.

Besides…if he completed this mission and regained his true identity, maybe, after a cooling-off period, he could get to know her again. Really know her. Not just physically.

But for now—

"It would be easier for me to make suggestions if you sent me an email from that system," she told him, no further humor in her voice. "Like, if you hadn't stolen my computer."

"I understand," he said. "But I'll tell you all I know about it, then you can tell me anything you think of that might let me access others' accounts."

So far, he had collected what information he could about the company's executives who put proposals together for government contracts, and who ultimately pushed for their acceptance and negotiated their contents. He now had a whole list of AFD people whose email accounts he wanted to see so he could review their communications with each other and, even more importantly, their communications with government employees—especially within the Corps of Engineers—while the contracts were under negotiation.

Somewhere, in all those emails, might be the information he sought: who had authorized shoddy work for prime monetary consideration—the issues he had started researching and revealing to his superiors while in Afghanistan…that damned information that had ultimately led to his "death."

The suggestions of his official techie contacts hadn't been much help yet.

"I don't suppose you'd just give me back my computer so I could handle this for you, would you, Jim?" Her voice now was low and seductive, as if she asked instead for him to return there for another night of hot sex.

Too bad that wasn't so. Or that he couldn't have agreed anyway. Too much was at stake.

."Sorry." He knew his tone didn't sound sorry at all. "I need to do this. But you're savvy enough to give me detailed instructions. So what are they?"

She laughed again. "I had to try. Anyway, here's what I'd suggest."

A lot of what she said made logical sense. Some he had her rephrase since his techie knowledge was limited. He made notes while keeping his ears open for anyone passing by.

When she was done, she said, "I'm not sure it'll work, Jim. But you can always call me with questions. I'll be here." She sounded wistful, and he wished he were close enough to kiss her lovely, hot lips in gratitude...and, with luck, seduction.

Instead, all he said was, "Thanks, Sally. I'll check in again later with Roy to make sure everything's all right. Meantime, you continue to listen to him. Okay?"

"Okay," she responded. The words she added, though, made him want even more to be with her. "Just take care of yourself, Jim. Stay safe. I'd really feel...well, I just don't want what the world thinks about you know who...never mind."

He knew what she'd wanted to say, though.

She didn't want the world thought about Brody McAndrews to actually come true.

Chapter 13

What Sherra did want, though, was to shake some sense into Brody.

She slammed the landline's receiver back into its cradle and stared at it, as if it still created a direct line to Brody through which she could attempt to reason with him.

She hadn't tried to make her instructions harder or more detailed than necessary, but they were still complicated to someone who didn't deal with complex computer research all the time.

Didn't he realize how much easier it would be for him to access the email if she jumped in and did the work? She had no idea whether what she'd said had gotten through to him.

What if he did hack into the company's email but created red flags within its security system? She'd tried to make that part clear to him, too, but what if she hadn't been specific enough?

She stood. No way could she just sit around doing nothing, or even merely using her own smart phone to do surreptitious research on Brody's behalf.

All she would do is worry about him and what waves he was creating—potentially dangerous ones.

She had already considered ways to get the hell out of this remote, if scenic, Dodge. Now she absolutely had to put the best plan into effect.

She glanced toward the living room doorway. No sign of Roy. Had he been watching her? Listening from nearby?

She needed to get his attention now.

She rocked forward from the waist, hugging herself around the belly. She moaned slightly—feigned, but she had to make it look good.

Then she hurried back toward her bedroom. Still no sign of Roy. She shut the door anyway, then ran into the bathroom, also slamming its door shut behind her.

She waited for five minutes, then emerged and again left her room. She walked slowly, as if in pain.

Roy was in the kitchen, sitting at the table with a glass of water in front of him. He was reading a magazine on hot rods.

Sherra doubled over, squeezing her midsection while taking deep breaths. When she straightened, she said, "I've got a problem, cousin. I need to go to a drugstore right away."

"No way," Roy said. "We're staying here till I hear otherwise from Brody or one of my commanding officers."

"Then I'll be in trouble and so will you. I won't go into detail, but I need some feminine products a lot earlier than anticipated this month, so I'm not prepared. I need them fast."

He stood and pushed the chair back so quickly that he appeared ready to run away. The guy didn't like to hear about female problems? Too bad.

"You don't have—I mean, can't you use something else?"

"Not considering…well, the extent of my problem. And it's likely to get worse. This has happened before, especially when I'm under stress. And you of all people should recognize that I am definitely under stress."

"All right," he finally said, unease scrunching wrinkles along his broad forehead. His face was florid, from his wide, flabby chin to the top of his bald head. "We'll make it quick as possible. And I'll need to be with you all the time."

She grinned almost wickedly. "In the aisle with feminine products? Sure." Then, for effect, she doubled over once more, clutched her stomach and groaned.

They drove to a large chain pharmacy in the closest retail area to the house.

It went better than Sherra had hoped. Cousin Roy was even more uncomfortable being around feminine products than he was being around a woman with female problems. He stayed an aisle or so away as she pretended to consider available choices.

Fortunately, Brody hadn't taken any belongings from her except those that might provide internet access—the ones he knew about. Her purse still contained her wallet, and it held a little cash and a credit card.

She bent down to ostensibly look at the items on the lower shelf…then quickly duckwalked away, staying low enough that her bodyguard couldn't see her.

Once outside, she hurried into a large grocery store. There, she pulled out her smart phone and used it to find a taxi service. To catch the cab without being seen, she chose a nearby busy strip mall. Could she get there in time and without Roy seeing her?

He would be searching for her. Was probably already looking, furious with her.

She managed it, though. It didn't hurt that she'd layered

her clothes and now stripped down to a whole different outfit—tank top and shorts instead of sweatshirt and jeans. Plus, she pinned up her shoulder-length black hair beneath a cap she had found at the house. Not a great disguise, but it was better than nothing.

She walked into the parking lot with shoulders hunched, legs slightly bent, trying to use an entirely different gait from her norm. Fortunately, she didn't see Roy. That didn't mean he hadn't seen her, but he didn't jump from behind any cars.

She didn't run but wove between cars, then ducked into a clothing store, followed by a liquor store, all the time watching for a pursuer.

She soon reached the strip mall. The cab was already there. She hurried inside and slammed the door.

Instead of giving her own address, many miles from here, she gave Brody's—which was just as far. She'd thought this through. Her condo wasn't safe. Plus, it would be easier to help Brody at his home.

And wouldn't it be fun to surprise him there similarly to the way he had burst into her place?

As the taxi drove off, Sherra spotted Roy for the first time. He was stomping furiously outside the pharmacy where they had last been together.

Fortunately, he didn't look in the taxi's direction.

She was free.

"What do you mean she disappeared?" Brody, fortunately alone in a hallway at AFD, was livid. He'd known from the moment he saw Roy's name and number on the caller ID that things couldn't be good—but this? He tightened his fist that wasn't holding the phone, half wishing it was around Roy's neck.

"She played me. I was stupid. I admit it."

As if Roy's admission would remedy the situation. "What do you mean?"

Hesitantly, the man told Brody what Sherra had said and done. "When I looked around in the drugstore, she was gone. I spent an hour looking for her everywhere, in that store and others nearby, but I couldn't find her."

If the situation wasn't so critical, Brody might have smiled about Sherra's creativity. But it was critical. He had taken her to the safe house to keep her...well, safe. Now, she could be in danger once more, and he didn't know how to find and protect her.

Assuming Roy was telling the truth.

Since Brody had her cell phone with him, he couldn't even call her.

"Keep looking—discreetly," he told Roy through clenched teeth. With nothing else to go on, Brody had to at least act as if he fully trusted Roy. The guy had been assigned by those in charge and had good security clearances. But that wasn't always enough. "Ask whether there are any buses that went through the area when you lost her, or if anyone saw a cab go by." Or she might just have hitched a ride with a stranger. What man in his right mind could resist a flirtatious woman as gorgeous as Sherra if she asked for transport?

Which only added to her potential peril. Even if the people he was protecting her from had no idea where she was, that wouldn't keep her from being harmed by some pervert rapist glad to give her the ride she'd asked for...and more.

"Find her," he finished and hung up. Assuming Roy was legitimate, Brody couldn't completely blame him. Sherra was smart and determined. And Brody was furious with her.

He was also furious that he didn't understand enough of her instructions to be able to hack into all the company email. Some, yes, but his success so far was limited.

He leaned back in his desk chair and stared at the computer monitor. He'd managed some hacking, at least. He had gotten into some fairly meaningless accounts of company underlings, and their messages over the past months only whetted his appetite to read their bosses' correspondence.

He'd seen questions about what had happened in Afghanistan on one of their current major projects.

He had seen other questions about possible discrepancies in data about who'd been killed there.

But the people whose accounts he'd gotten into were peons charged with finding information, not giving the orders that had led to what had happened. Or even securing the jobs overseas that had given rise to the discrepancies he had discovered and started investigating there.

So far, he was stymied. But he had to get through, get more information—even faster, now, than he had planned.

For now he had another problem.

He had to find Sherra and make sure she stayed safe.

The weather was drizzly, not surprising for May. Watching cars speed past on the highway heading toward Washington, D.C., Sherra tried to keep her mind on how happy she was about her escape without admitting to the dreariness compounded by the weather that washed inside her.

She'd been successful in getting away, but whatever lay before her wouldn't all be pretty.

Still, facing Brody's wrath was better than hiding and not knowing what was going on. Or failing to help him and hearing about all that went wrong afterward.

At least the cabby had a middle-of-the-road music station on. The soft rock helped to bolster her mood a bit.

It was a good thing that she had been nosy—well, interested. She had wanted to see what Brody's fake IDs had looked like, so she had sneaked a look at his wallet one night when he was in the shower.

One Maryland driver's license resembled hers, of course, for the address in Glen Burnie, Maryland, under his fake name of Bill Bradshaw.

The other, Jim Martin, had a different address, in Washington—probably an apartment building, since it had a unit number.

She had been wise enough to copy it down. She'd also copied Cousin Ray's number from Brody's smart phone, in case she thought she needed a bodyguard later. She had scrolled down Brody's list of numbers to see who else was there, too—like herself.

This taxi ride would cost a fortune but would be worth it. She just hoped she could be as resourceful as Brody had been and find a way to get inside to wait for him.

She wasn't fleeing him, after all—just his control over her life. And now she needed his help to get her life back.

Acting sick again wasn't Brody's favorite idea. But he was too keyed up to delve much more into the AFD computer system. He might make a mistake.

One that could prove fatal.

Instead, leaning forward, elbows planted on his desk, he called Crandall Forbes on the company phone system. He held his forehead tightly with the hand that didn't grip the phone. There weren't windows into Crandall's office so he couldn't see him, but acting sick would make his upcoming pretense easier to maintain.

When his supervisor answered, Brody made his voice as nasal as possible. "Sorry, boss. I thought I was feeling better, but—" He started to cough.

"Did you sort those latest resumes for the project in the Philippines?" Crandall demanded.

"Yes, and there are a few that stand out. I'll email them to you. I want to finish a couple more odds and ends today, too, but is it okay if I leave early?"

It was just past lunchtime and Brody hadn't had a break. Hadn't wanted one. His idea of leaving early today would only involve his hanging around for less than an hour.

"Yeah, go ahead. In fact, take a few more days and get over the damned thing."

"I think if I just go home and sleep for a few hours I'll be fine to come in tomorrow." He didn't want to take more time off. He needed to be here for the best likelihood of prying into the upper echelon's emails. But he left the door open just in case—since he didn't know how long it would take to find Sherra and ensure that, this time, she really would stay in one place and remain safe. "If not, I'll call and leave you a message. I really appreciate this. Sorry I'm being such a sickly wimp. I'm taking lots of vitamins and all so it shouldn't happen again."

He wasn't really sorry. That wimpy attitude fit well with who he pretended to be here in the human resources department of AFD. With luck, no one would ever suspect that someone as mousy and obedient as he appeared could ever hack into company records—let alone his real identity.

They would find that out eventually, though. He would enjoy shocking them all when he'd figured out the identities of those he sought and had all the evidence he needed to put them away forever.

He turned back to the computer. One more go at it, then he was out of here.

Sherra winced as she swiped the credit card through the cab's reader. At least the D.C. neighborhood where Brody lived looked decent, and there were plenty of stores, including coffee shops, around. She could hang out there if she failed to get inside.

"Thanks," she said to the driver, took her receipt from him, and exited the cab.

The building was bland-looking, which undoubtedly fit with Brody's cover. Nothing elite for Jim Martin, the down-to-earth low-level employee trying to make ends meet on a peon's salary, she supposed, paid by a major defense contracting company. He'd have to hide all his real skills there and play at being a nobody.

One of those coffee shops, a national chain, was right next door. Another apartment building sat on the other side, and several matching ones stretched down the street.

At least the drizzle had stopped, and although the air remained humid it was on the cool side. It was midafternoon, and only a few other people were on the sidewalk in this mostly residential neighborhood. Cars crawled by on the street, though. This was part of Washington, D.C., with all its crowded glory.

Moving up the sidewalk, Sherra approached the glass double doors. She noticed the phone off to the side where visitors could call residents for entry.

The resident she sought wasn't home, but she scanned the list on the attached chart. Good. There was a number for the manager.

She edged closer to the phone as a few people ambled down the street past her. She pressed the appropriate numbers and waited as the phone rang.

"Building manager," droned a female voice. "How can I help you?"

"My name is Sally Bradshaw," Sherra said in a high-pitched voice. "I'm Jim Martin's girlfriend. I don't live around here, though, and just arrived from out of town.

It's a surprise. Could you let me into his apartment?" She gave the number.

"Sorry, Ms. Bradshaw. That's against company policy. Why don't you go next door for some coffee to wait? Better yet, call your boyfriend. Whatever works best."

What'd work best would be your cooperation, Sherra thought. But she'd known it was a long shot.

"Thanks," she said with no enthusiasm and hung up. Maybe she would grab a cup of coffee while deciding what to do next.

"Ms. Bradshaw?" said another female voice from behind her—one with a Southern accent, so it wasn't the manager she'd just spoken with.

Sherra turned. Three people stood there—two men and a woman, whom she'd noticed walking down the street. She looked around, uneasy. Other pedestrians were nearby, and still a lot of cars on the street. Surely someone would help her if something was wrong.

Why were these people standing there? Why had they paid attention to her name?

"Yes," she admitted tentatively.

The woman took a step toward her. She appeared middle-age and wore a blouse with a frilly collar over a midlength gray skirt. She didn't look threatening, but Sherra had been through enough lately not to feel assured by appearances.

"My name is Mae Andrews," she said.

Sherra blinked. Andrews? As in the dead, other Brody?

"This is my husband, Burl, and son Bobby," she continued. "I know it sounds strange, but I just heard you ask about Jim Martin. We have reason to believe that he's—well, it's a long, strange story. Would you join us for a cup of coffee?" She pointed to the coffee shop. "We're looking for some information, and even if you don't have it you might still be able to help. Please?"

Chapter 14

"Are you really Jim Martin's girlfriend?" asked Burl Andrews.

The four of them sat around a small table at the coffee shop. Sherra had gotten a latte with lots of sweetener. She needed the energy pickup along with the caffeine.

Mae had chosen an iced tea, and both Burl and Bobby had ordered brewed coffee. It seemed a toss-up who had poured more milk and sugar into it.

Burl was a thin man, lots of wrinkles on his face that didn't quite meet his receding hairline. Appearing to be in his sixties, he regarded Sherra expectantly while awaiting her answer.

Unsure what to say, she responded with a question of her own. "I'd like to know what this is about," she said. "Why are you interested in Jim?"

"Because that's not who he is," Bobby responded bluntly. With thick glasses and ample, curly brown hair, he looked more like a computer geek than Sherra, or even her friend from CMHealthfoods, Miles, did. That didn't mean he was one, though.

"What do you mean?" Sherra's heart hammered an uneven cadence inside her chest. Brody's cover was blown, and by people who claimed to have the last name of Andrews?

What if they actually were relatives of the Brody Andrews who had been killed? Did they know he was dead?

Maybe these people believed the official, untrue story that Brody McAndrews was the victim—and that their son and brother remained alive.

If so, she felt sorry for them.

But still—what were they doing here? How did they know that the fictitious Jim Martin was involved?

"We don't really know what's going on." Mae, sounding depressed, stared at her paper cup. "If you know Jim, maybe you can help us." She looked up at Sherra. "Who are you?" She had blond, wavy hair. Her eyes were light blue, surrounded by worry lines, and looked infinitely sad.

"My name is Sally," Sherra said. "And, yes, I know Jim. What do you want with him?"

Burl half stood. "This isn't getting us anywhere. Look, Sally, we need answers, and you're going to give them to us." He'd been sitting beside Sherra and appeared ready to grab her. Damn. She'd thought she would be safe out here in public while she tried to figure this out. But she was way over her head in this situation. She needed Brody.

First, though, she needed information. "What answers are you looking for?" she asked sweetly.

Mae sighed. "We need to know where our son Brody is."

Although Sherra tried not to move even an eyelash as she waited for more, she was trembling.

"My brother was in Afghanistan." Bobby looked as angry as his dad. "We've been told he's back in the States on a super secret mission but we haven't heard from him. We want to make sure he's okay."

"I got an email from someone in the government," Mae said. "It said Brody was undercover here in the D.C. area,. We probably shouldn't have, but after we still didn't hear from Brody we hired a private investigator to try to find him. He told us he'd learned that Brody was using the name Jim Martin and that he lived right here. We were just about to try that apartment building when we heard you mention that name."

Sherra decided to tell them that the Jim Martin she knew couldn't be the same one. This family, their claims and the amazing coincidence of their timing didn't feel right to her. Not that she was an expert on clandestine stuff. But she knew someone who was.

"That's very interesting," she said noncommittally, then glanced at her watch. "Look, I'm supposed to meet someone in a little while and I'm going to be late. Excuse me for a second while I call and let him know."

She stood abruptly and walked away. If these people were the real Brody Andrews's family, she could be blowing things for her Brody. If not, he needed to know about them. She walked outside onto the sidewalk and watched them as she drew her personal smart phone out of her purse. Under these circumstances, maybe Brody would forgive her for not telling him about it. Or not. It didn't really matter.

She pressed in his number as the people at the table continued to watch her.

Where the hell was she?

Brody had dashed from AFD to Sherra's condo and let himself in the same way he had the first time. The place was empty.

He stood in her kitchen now, looking for any indication

she might have come here and run off again. But as far as he could tell no one had been here since they'd left.

He sank into a kitchen chair to think but was too edgy to stay still. Instead, he rose and hurried down the hall to the bedroom she used as an office. No sign of her presence there, either. He booted up her desktop computer but had no idea what to look for.

He also had no idea where else Sherra might flee to after leaving the safe house. Maybe she had left the area altogether. Gone to Baltimore-Washington Airport and taken the first flight to Fiji or wherever.

He should never have allowed her to keep one of her own credit cards, but she'd promised to use it only in an emergency. How easy could that be when she didn't have her own ID with her? And even if her driver's license in the name of Sally Bradshaw got her somewhere, she didn't have a passport.

Damn! Didn't she know how much danger she was in? She had to—she had been attacked right here.

Which might, he reasoned as he sat down at her computer, be exactly why she wasn't here now.

Where else would she go?

He made himself breathe slowly as he scanned her computer files, but nothing seemed helpful. He wanted to kick himself for leaving her without a phone—only, he had done that for her protection.

His phone rang, vibrating in his pocket. He grabbed it and pulled it out.

He didn't recognize the number. The first thing that ran through his mind was that someone had Sherra and was calling to gloat.

Someone who might already have harmed her...

"Hello," he answered abruptly.

"Hi, Bill," said a sweet, familiar voice that made him stand so abruptly that the chair flew backward behind him.

"Sally. Where—"

"Do you happen to remember Jim Martin? I'm right outside his apartment building, and there are some people who claim he may not be who he says he is. Their name is Andrews, and I'm having coffee with them at the shop next door. I—"

"Stay right there," Brody demanded, pushing the button to turn off the computer and dashing for the door. "In public. With people around. I'll be right there."

Brody drove like a maniac along the beltway from Bethesda toward downtown D.C. He had to get back to the apartment he was renting. Fast.

Could they really be the Andrewses? What was Sherra telling them?

He grabbed his phone and pushed in the number for Michael Cortez. He spoke to his commanding officer daily to keep him up to date. Now, he was the one who needed to be brought up to date.

"What's up...is it Jim today?" The captain had answered right away, his tone full of good humor. As if what was going on wasn't damned serious.

"Right. I need to know immediately if you or one of your staff can find out where 'my' family, the Andrewses, happen to be right now. Check with Ragar—he mentioned they were nosing around. As I recall, my parents are Mae and Burl and I have a brother." Once he had known he was going to have to assume the other Brody's identity for a while, or at least make it appear as if that Brody had been the survivor, Brody McAndrews had done his homework. Learned that the other Brody had grown up in Atlanta. Where he had gone to school. Who his family members were. When and where he had enlisted.

He'd nailed the basics, in case anyone ever interrogated him to confirm his identity.

He was fortunate it hadn't happened before. Now, he wasn't certain whether he would have to pretend he had no idea what the real Andrews family was talking about—or make sure that, whoever they were, he brought them down before they could hurt Sherra or him or his cover.

"That's right. Bobby. I'll talk to Ragar and have one of my guys do a quick recon on them, too. Why do you need to know?"

Brody filled him in quickly on Sherra's escape from the safe house—and her call to him.

Where had she gotten a phone so quickly? Was it one of those limited-use things from a convenience store?

He was just glad she had it.

"I'm on my way now. It'd help to know whether those claiming to be the Andrewses actually could be them. Either way, I'm damned concerned about why they happen to be at Jim Martin's place. My cover may be blown even more than I'd thought."

Their talking freely on the phone was unlikely to make things worse, at least—not with the way the system was configured with protections built in.

"I'll get back to you as soon as possible," Michael said. "One way or the other, this'll ramp up the urgency of your mission even more. Have you gotten into the emails of the company execs yet?"

"Working on it. The suggestions your tech guys provided helped me past the lower rungs of security, but not all I needed. I don't want to make it obvious that someone is trying to bypass what's in place, either, so this process is even slower than physically tagging after people to learn what I could."

"So what's your plan?"

"I've got another source I'm tapping into for advice," he said obscurely.

"Yeah? I can guess who that source is." Brody couldn't tell if Michael approved or not. His tone was sardonic, though—in amusement or anger?

"Maybe you can, and maybe—"

"Your Sherra has already proven that she can stick her nose nearly anywhere on the internet, so go for it," Michael said. "Only problem was, what she does is detectable to those with good skills or you wouldn't be on her case. Better do it fast and right the first time."

Michael disconnected before Brody could agree—or express concern.

Brody soon reached his exit and got off the Beltway. His apartment was only a couple of miles farther.

How would he handle this?

Smoothly. It had to be done right. Whether these people were the real Andrewses or not, they could be as eager to make contact with him as he was with them at this moment.

They might have information he could use.

If so, he'd make sure they turned it over. Without harming Sherra or him.

He only hoped she was okay.

As Brody parked the car, Michael called back. "My sources say that the Andrewses have been making waves. They don't get why their son hasn't been in touch, even while on some covert assignment. They apparently hired a private investigator who somehow unearthed a connection with 'Jim Martin,' so they may assume that, when Jim Martin appears, it'll be their son. Treat 'em as gently as you can. It sounds legit."

"Thanks." Brody hung up to finish parking. This promised to be an interesting meeting.

But even with this additional tidbit of info, he wouldn't let down his guard.

Sherra was glad—and relieved—to see Brody enter the store. He stalked in and looked around with such intensity that she wondered if he would be the one to cause a scene. But as he caught her eye, he scrunched over into his Jim Martin character—noticeable to her, but she doubted anyone else would catch the instantaneous transformation.

Despite the crowd filling nearly all the coffee shop's tables, he reached them fairly quickly. All eyes at her table were on him.

Except hers. Sherra looked from Mae to Burl to Bobby, wondering what their expressions meant. None appeared to recognize Brody, which wasn't surprising. Did that mean they actually were who they'd said—Brody Andrews's family? They most likely wouldn't have met the man with the similar name to their relative.

Sherra had been friendly but not disclosing as they waited for "Jim." Now, she would let him take the lead.

He approached her first. "Hi, Sally. Good to see you."

He gave no indication of who they were supposed to pretend to be to one another, so she kept things general, too. "Hi, Jim. Glad to see you, too, but I'm a bit confused about what's going on."

The three Andrewses stood, and so did Sherra. "You're Jim Martin?" Burl demanded. His thin face looked florid, his mouth a straight line of disbelief.

"That's right." Brody sounded calm and he regarded the three people with friendly interest. "And you are…"

"We're the Andrewses." Mae's voice sounded sad and strained. She chewed her bottom lip as if to gnaw away the urge to cry, then continued, "We got some inaccurate information, I'm afraid. We thought—"

"We thought you were my brother in disguise," Bobby finished as his mother's words tapered off. His expression was blank, as if he had shuttered all emotion, unlike his parents.

So were these people who they'd claimed to be? Sherra had doubted it before, but they seemed so genuine.

"Sorry." Brody sounded as if he meant it. He, too, must believe in them.

"Look, we're just so confused," Mae continued. "Would you mind coming with us to someplace quiet—a lounge, maybe, where we can get a drink? We'll tell you what's been happening. I doubt you'll be able to help, but maybe you can tell us why your name came up when we started trying to find our son."

Sherra looked at Brody for a cue. Was he willing to go along?

She doubted it. Even if they were the real family of poor Brody Andrews, it could hurt Brody's cover if he let on that he knew anything about their dead son and brother.

She was surprised, then, when he agreed. "I don't think we can help," he said, "but we'll join you for a drink."

Good sob story, Brody thought, moving around the table to be closest to Sherra. He took her arm, giving a warning glance that she apparently understood since her questioning expression turned bland.

"You're here early for dinner, dear," he told her, giving her a hint of the persona she should take on. Jim's girlfriend should be a good, benign role.

He didn't want these folks to be the real family of Brody Andrews. He didn't want to meet the real Andrewses until he had found, with certainty, who was behind the assault in Afghanistan that had led to the other Brody's death. He wanted to be able to hand them that, at least, to help them reach closure.

They certainly made it look good, though. He'd have to be careful what he said, just in case.

Hadn't Brody Andrews told him his mother had straight gray hair? That could have been changed, of course.

If they weren't the real Andrewses, he needed to learn who they were and get them to reveal who had sent them here.

He knew where to take them for the quiet discussion they requested.

He'd just have to figure out how to get Sherra safely out of the way, and then he would elicit the truth. Whatever it took.

Chapter 15

Brody had done his homework. After moving to this neighborhood in the guise of a human resources underling at AFD, he had acted like a regular guy—part of the role he played.

That meant checking out local restaurants and bars. He'd even pretended to flirt with local women, although he had kept that to a minimum.

But he'd made mental note of which places were best for maintaining anonymity, and which had the friendliest staff.

He therefore led this group toward The Drinking Place, a mellow bar down the street. Its main evening bartender had become a buddy of sorts, or at least a tentative ally.

Brody could rely on Kern to keep an eye on things. They had talked enough for Brody to find out that Kern was once in the military—Special Forces like Brody's own brother—and although Brody admitted to nothing, he knew the guy had figured out that Brody was more than he seemed.

They talked now and then and said little, but Brody believed they had bonded beneath the surface.

He might be about to find out for sure.

Brody thought he could at least trust Kern to call the cops if things went south. In fact, a few cops frequented The Drinking Place now and then, although it was probably too early for them to appear.

His arm was around Sherra's shoulders as he ushered the group down the street. He liked the feeling, even though they were both just playing roles again. She looked up at him now and then as if trying to figure out what he was thinking.

A good thing. Maybe she would follow his lead.

The supposed family members seemed inclined to lag behind, but Brody wouldn't let them. He held Sherra back, pointing out stores, restaurants and places of quasi-interest, as if the others were tourists and he wanted to ensure they had a good time.

Not that they appeared to have any interest. But even if they were the Andrewses that wasn't surprising.

The Drinking Place was only a couple of blocks from the coffee shop, and the group soon arrived. Brody let the others enter first, then preceded Sherra and pointed to a sufficiently large table at one side of the dark, nearly empty venue.

He nodded toward the bartender, glad to see that it was indeed Kern on duty. He'd slip away from the table in a bit, ostensibly to check on their order. That way, he'd have a moment alone with the guy to give him a heads-up that this group might not be all that it seemed.

A familiar barmaid—tall, leggy and attentive—in a skimpy uniform approached their table. She been Brody's server before and began to flirt with him as the others gave their orders.

He played along to see Sherra's reaction.

"I want the same thing my guy is having." Sherra sent a pseudo-dreamy glance his way.

The barmaid, whose name Brody had never ascertained because it was irrelevant to him, shot him an angry glare as she waited for his order. He smiled benignly—and ordered a heavy dark ale that he doubted Sherra would enjoy, based on his recollections of her preferences in the past.

Not that he'd drink it, or at least not all of it and definitely not fast. He needed his wits about him.

But he enjoyed the annoyed glance Sherra leveled on him before he looked again at the Andrewses. Unsurprisingly—maybe for the roles they played—Mae ordered a glass of wine, and the two men ordered gin and tonics, heavy on the gin.

As they waited, Brody prompted them. "I'd like to hear what's going on—what brought you here looking for me." As Jim. This could be interesting.

They gave a damned good spiel as if they were really the Andrewses. Maybe they were. If so, Brody felt sorry for them. He wished, in some ways, that they had actually found their son undercover here, at the end of their quest. When he'd been recruited for this mission, he had fought to get someone to tell both families the truth, his and the Andrewses, as long as they all promised to keep it to themselves. But those in charge didn't agree. They claimed it wasn't in the best interests of national security, and maybe it wasn't. They also said this would give Brody the impetus to fulfill his mission as fast as possible.

If these folks weren't really Brody Andrews's family, who were they—and why were they here?

"The PI we hired assured us that the person named Jim Martin who lived in your building was really our son," Burl said. He looked around as if wishing his drink was already in his hands. "We'd already been told by someone in the military—a guy who stayed anonymous—that Brody was on a very special secret mission and had to go undercover here in the States. But we haven't heard from him in months, so we decided to try to find him. We've been hanging around a couple of days, but Jim wasn't here—till now."

"I understand." Sherra sounded wistful. Brody felt certain she was remembering her own quest after hearing he'd died.

He wished that didn't make his insides start looping to warm and fuzzy.

He stood abruptly. "Excuse me. I'm going to check on our order." He felt Sherra's irritation once more, but so be it.

It was early enough that the bar wasn't too crowded, so he was able to motion to Kern to approach in an area far from where people were seated.

"Everything okay, Jim?" The guy's voice was perennially raspy, as if he yelled a lot over conversations in this establishment. His body had gone to flab beneath his white shirt and black trousers, and a requisite apron was carelessly tied around his waist. "Your drinks'll be served in a minute."

"Fine." Brody drew closer. "I'd like you to keep watch on my group tonight. I have a feeling…" He didn't finish but felt certain Kern would get it.

He did. Drawing even closer, he said in a low voice, "Something covert? Anyone you'll need for me to call?"

"The cops should be good enough if anything goes down that shouldn't. Hopefully it won't."

Kern nodded and stepped back. Louder, he said, "I'll make sure your beer is really cold this time. Sorry about last time you were here."

Brody would have to buy him a beer sometime. Or maybe just fill him in when this miserable excuse for a civilian exercise was over—anything he could reveal then, at least.

He returned to the table. Mae Andrews was speaking earnestly with Sherra, telling her how strange things had been since they were notified about their Brody's covert assignment. "We didn't even know he was going into that side of the military. Before, he'd seemed happy to just be an army private. But I can't tell you how proud of him we are."

The server brought their drinks a minute after Brody resumed his seat. His beer really was cold. He held up the bottle to salute Kern who was, unsurprisingly, watching them.

They stayed for another half hour. Bobby described how he'd checked with some military contacts about his brother's supposed assignment, then, feeling dissatisfied, had contacted the PI. The detective had come across the name Jim Martin and the D.C. location but otherwise hit a dead end.

He had obviously been wrong, the Andrewses all agreed. Jim Martin was definitely not Brody Andrews.

Sherra acted as if she bought it all. She listened closely, her lovely face appearing sad and sympathetic. He knew she could be good actress, but this seemed real.

Which only made him feel more bummed out, since he was starting to buy it, too.

Plus, he was damned worried that any nosy person, PI or not, could associate Brody Andrews with Jim Martin. Was his assignment in trouble again?

"Sorry to bend your ear this way," Mae finally finished. Burl plopped a couple of bills on the table, and Brody paid for Sherra's drink and his own. "It helps to talk about it, though. I don't suppose you really know anything about where our Brody is, do you?"

She regarded "Jim" hopefully, and he shook his head. "I wish I did," he said, knowing that he might, someday, have to tell these people he'd been lying and he was fully aware that their son was killed in action in Afghanistan.

Under other circumstances, the death of Brody Andrews would not have been covered up this way. He only hoped that it would be clear he had saved other lives by the oper-

ation he conducted, so that Brody's death hadn't been obscured in vain.

Outside the bar, they all started walking down the sidewalk once more. It was more crowded now, later in the
evening.

"We're parked over there." Burl pointed to a lot between
two restaurants. "Look, I've got couple more questions.
Would you mind heading there with us?"

Brody did mind but still wanted to know what they were
up to. He considered ordering "Sally" back to his place, but
discarded the idea. First, he didn't want her to be alone in
case this was a ruse for someone to break into his apartment
and search it while he was preoccupied—not that they'd find
anything helpful there.

And second, they might not do whatever they had in mind
if the two of them separated.

Third, and probably most important, was that Sherra
would not obey his order unless she agreed with it up front.

So, Brody would do what he had to and learn what the
Andrewses wanted to say.

Mostly, he would stay wary.

Sherra sensed Brody's mistrust. She felt it, too.

As a result, she was a little surprised he agreed to ac-
company the Andrewses to the parking lot.

It was well-lit, at least. But it looked crowded with cars
and nearly devoid of people. Not the safest place to go if
these folks really were here to shut down Brody's assignment—by shutting him down physically.

She trusted him. She would be careful and follow his
leads.

Her walking beside Mae seemed okay with Brody. The
older woman talked a lot about her son growing up in the
South, how close they were, the works. She was laying it on

thick. If this wasn't real, these people must be extra skilled in putting their targets off guard. Or trying to.

They reached the parking lot. An attendant's booth stood near the entrance.

"Sorry we couldn't be more help," Brody said. "Sally, it's time for you to head off on the errand you told me about. I'll meet you at my place."

That errand was in his imagination. Clearly Brody didn't want Sherra to go farther into the shadow-filled lot.

She didn't want him to, either. Not if he might be in danger. "Come with me," she said. "Nice talking to all of you."

Only they weren't all together any longer. Mae had turned and unlocked a nearby aging white sedan with a Georgia license plate. She slid into the driver's seat.

"Get into the car," said Bobby, who was closest to Sherra. His tone was menacing, and when Sherra turned she saw he was holding a gun.

So was Burl.

"What's this about?" Brody demanded. "Who are you really? What do you want?"

He took a step toward Sherra as if to protect her. Even as Jim Martin, who had an apparent romantic interest in the woman he referred to as Sally, that was no surprise.

The next thing was, though. Brody whipped out his own gun and immediately shot Burl. Fortunately, Burl didn't get off a shot but shrieked in pain as he fell to the ground, clutching his chest. Brody grabbed his gun.

Mae screamed and aimed the car toward Brody, but he dove out of the way, aiming his gun toward Bobby.

He gave a quick, grim nod toward Sherra, and she knew what he wanted. She threw herself to the pavement and tried to get out of the way. But Bobby grabbed her and drew her up, still holding the gun on her. "Like I said, get into the car." He didn't seem at all perturbed about what had happened.

Sherra glanced around in a panic. She saw people start toward the parking lot. That bartender was one of them, the one Brody appeared to know. He had a phone in his hand.

"Nope," she said. She acted as if she was about to go limp, but then drew herself up and kicked him hard, where it really should hurt.

He grabbed himself and her, too, as he fell to the ground writhing. She knew she was supposed to be his shield from Brody, and didn't like that in the least. She turned and started pummeling him in the face as well as the groin. His grip on the gun loosened and she somehow managed to pull it away.

By then, cops started arriving. They took control of the situation quickly, separating Sherra from Brody, and the supposed Andrewses from each other, too.

Burl appeared bloody but alive. Bobby was clearly in pain, and Sherra could only smile at that.

At least it was over.

Brody called Michael Cortez from the sidewalk outside the police station that evening, before he went inside to answer questions.

Sherra was with him. She was okay, no thanks to him. He should have been more insistent. He should have—well, he would talk to her later about it.

"Get someone good to interrogate them fast," Brody told Michael over the phone. "We need to know who knows what, and whose orders they acted under."

Michael promised to do what he could.

Even so, when Brody hung up he felt furious and powerless.

Until Sherra drew closer and put her arms around him. She stood on tiptoes, kissed him on the mouth, then whispered, "We can get some answers, at least. I happen to have grabbed dear Bobby's cell phone—and we should be able to trace his calls."

Chapter 16

It was getting late by the time Brody and Sherra were free to go, after their respective interrogations.

Cops and civilians passed them as they waited at curbside for a cab outside the modern concrete police facility.

Pulling his phone from his pocket, Brody called Captain Cortez again. "We're out. All seemed okay from this end. Any information yet?"

"I'm still looking into it. Do the cops know anything they shouldn't that I'll need to smooth out?"

"My identity never became an issue," Brody said. Which was fortunate. The ID that had been created for him as Jim Martin had worked. He hadn't had to take local authorities aside to explain who he really was and why Jim Martin had been created.

Whatever the putative Andrews family members knew, they hadn't spoken about it, either, or about anything else. "Burl" was in a local hospital under constant guard until well enough to be booked at the local police station as "Bobby" and "Mae" had been. Not that the local cops were likely to reveal all to someone who'd been involved and was therefore a potential witness, but Brody had overheard enough to believe that they had remained anonymous and silent so far. The suspects hadn't even denied that both unregistered weapons were theirs.

Brody would find a way to learn exactly who they were—and who had sent them. They were fortunate in some ways to remain incarcerated. They had knowledge he needed, and he'd have done all he could to extract it.

Especially since they had attempted to harm Sherra.

He wanted to kiss Sherra silly, both because she was unharmed, and because she had been smart and cunning enough to steal Bobby's cell phone even as he was trying to abduct her. She had it hidden now, and it hadn't been confiscated. Never mind that her stealing possible evidence was illegal. Brody would protect her.

But he still hated this situation. As soon as he could, he would extract her from it again, even if that meant putting her into some kind of witness protection program—which he knew she would fight all the way.

She was much too involved, too much in danger—and too close to him. Things seemed even more complicated now. He needed her out of this situation—and out of his life.

For the sanity and safety of both of them.

He would enjoy her nearness for the moment, though, even as he kept her safe.

"Where are we going?" Sherra whispered, sidling even closer, although he kept one arm around her to ensure her nearness and security. He soon saw why. They had avoided talking to the media at the attack scene, but those buzzards still hovered around the police station. Sherra and he had been seen, and a couple approached with cameras and microphones ready to attack.

"I'll tell you when we're on our way." He moved in front of her as protection but was glad to see the taxi he'd called stop at the curb near them.

He opened the door for Sherra and let her in before sliding beside her. He gave Jim Martin's home address to the attentive driver, who immediately programmed it into his GPS.

"That's where we're going?" Sherra asked as they started off. She glanced significantly toward the driver, then said, "But people will think to look for us there."

Brody appreciated that she gave no details that could be overheard. "Right, but we need my car for transportation. I'll make sure there's no tracking device on it, and there are ways of staying elusive."

"Are we going back to the safe house?"

"I'm not sure if it's still safe," he said with a humorless laugh. "We still don't know who those goons were or who sent them. No, wherever we wind up, it'll be a place no one knows about."

The taxi dropped them off a few minutes later. Brody paid cash, then scanned the area. The sidewalk near his apartment building was empty, although there were some pedestrians outside the nearby coffee shop and other retail establishments despite the late hour. He quickly led Sherra through the lobby to the garage.

There, he did a quick scan of his car for any electronic gadget that shouldn't be attached. Finding none, he popped open the trunk. He extracted another service weapon and a laptop.

"Hey—is that mine?" Sherra asked.

"Yeah, I brought it when I left you with Roy. Your phone, too, to make sure you couldn't use either. The computer's another reason we came back here. It's easier than buying a new one without using a credit card that can be traced. I don't like it, but I'm going to put you to work as long as I'm with you to observe. Let's go."

He drove the car defensively, turning corners fast and without signaling and otherwise conducting maneuvers designed to reveal if anyone was following them.

All looked good.

He drove them to a cheap chain motel on the city's outskirts, where he booked a room and paid cash. Since they checked in without luggage, he figured any curious employee would assume they were there for a short fling.

Maybe they were—along with needing a place to hide out.

They got key cards and walked up the steps to their second-floor room. It was compact but clean, with a queen-size bed dominating its decor.

Sherra immediately headed for the long window at its far end and pulled the curtains open. Then she sat on the bed facing the glass.

She extracted a phone from her purse—the one she had shown him before. It was the smart phone she had so smoothly lifted from Bobby as they fought.

"I've been dying of curiosity," she said. "It's time to learn who at least one of those nasty characters has been talking with. Sit here." She patted the bed beside her, which got Brody's body reacting. Not that he would do anything about his inevitable attraction to Sherra.

Later, though…

"I'll need to see if you recognize any of the numbers he's called recently that aren't connected with names he has programmed in," Sherra continued. "Okay?"

"Okay," he confirmed, and kept his kiss, as he joined her, agonizingly brief.

* * *

Sherra started the process the easy way. She was some-what familiar with this brand of smart phone, and she pressed icons on the screen until she found a list of contacts.

"No one here named Mae or Burl," she told Brody, who sat closely beside her on the side of the bed observing the phone over her shoulder as he kept one arm around her.

Too close. It was hard to concentrate. But she didn't want to brush him off and move away…yet. It felt too good. Plus, she'd been shaken by their encounter with the fake An-drewses, the fight and the ensuing police interview. A small bit of snuggling, for just a short while, could help.

Even so, Sherra was glad that the drapery stayed open. She couldn't see much besides the concrete wall at the far side of the narrow balcony, with the darkening sky above. Light bouncing off a conglomeration of puffy clouds pro-vided some illumination, but the rest came from their motel room.

There were other buildings around, and with their mod-icum of backlighting people might be able to see at least their outlines.

Which meant that, at least for the moment, their close-ness could not turn into anything more exciting. At least not until Brody closed the drapes for security—not that they were likely to have been followed here.

"Give the guy some credit for intelligence," Brody mur-mured into her ear so closely that it gave her shivers. "Try 'Mom' and 'Dad.'"

But neither those words nor any similar ones were on the list. Nor were there any Andrewses, or even any last names with the initial *A*.

Sherra scrolled down slowly, holding it in front of Brody. "I'm not likely to recognize names but why don't you take a look?"

When Brody shook his head negatively as the list progressed, she felt it. Why would something like that make her insides stir, as if he were touching her intimately, turning her on?

Maybe because they sat on a bed in a motel room. But moving away wouldn't buy her anything but more time with no answers.

When she reached the end, she changed the settings. "Here. This way the numbers are listed in the first column. See if you recognize any." She hesitated. "You might want to check them against numbers on your own phone that you've recently called, or those you've received."

He shifted, as if she'd irritated him. Maybe so, but she had to suggest it. "You think we have friends in common?" he asked derisively. "Hell, I know what you mean. And you're right. What I'm peeved about isn't what you said, but the fact that I don't know yet who's been playing me that way."

He took the phone and began scrolling down it himself. She watched, her gaze moving from his face to the numbers and back. He scowled but said nothing. Nor did he appear to focus on one number any more than the others.

He'd only scrolled through a portion of the screen when his own cell rang. He handed the one they'd been studying back to Sherra, then rose and walked away with his phone.

She immediately missed his closeness, which was silly. But she had to wait, for now, until he returned to follow up on reviewing the numbers.

Or not. She made a mental note of the numbers on the screen where Brody had stopped scrolling and continued looking herself.

She stopped at one near the end. It looked familiar—didn't it? She didn't know whose it was but believed she knew where it came from.

She had seen ones with a similar area code and first three digits on Brody's phone.

She'd have to wait and ask Brody after his current conversation ended. If she was right, he would want the information she might be able to grab for him.

He was apparently prepared to let her use her computer— but only in his company?

For the work he wanted her to do?

That was better than nothing, at least.

And she could always try to play games of her own.

"Did you find out anything about the Andrews pretenders yet?" Brody asked immediately, moving toward the bathroom and keeping his voice low. Force of habit, since what he expected to hear from Michael Cortez wouldn't be worthy of keeping secret from Sherra. Or trying to.

"Still working on it," the captain said. "But look. I know things have been strained for you over the past couple of days, but there've been rumblings around here that something is about to go down at AFD. We need you there tomorrow to check it out. Make sure you're over your cold. Got it? And if you happen to finally reach a breakthrough on who's communicating with what government branch, that would come in damned handy." He paused. "It's time you had a breakthrough, you know."

"Yeah. I know. Especially if I get an indication that anyone there was involved in the fake Andrewses situation. But about tomorrow, I need some more time." He hated saying that. He really did want to be at AFD, back in his undercover role, to be there particularly if there was something happening.

But protecting Sherra came first. And right now, he didn't even know what he could do with her, where he could put her that would be safe, if he wasn't around her.

"There's no time to give you, Jim." Michael's soft but unyielding voice emphasized the name in Brody's undercover ID pertaining to AFD. "You want someone else to wind up dead because you didn't get answers in time—ones just waiting for you to dig a little?"

"No." Brody knew his tone was abrupt and inappropriate for addressing his commanding officer, but he was damned unhappy with the situation. *Damned* was the right word. He might be damned if he failed to go there and see what the hell Michael was talking about.

He might be even more damned if he went there, leaving Sherra someplace that may or may not be safe, and something happened to her.

Although…what if he called Roy, got Sherra's former caretaker and bodyguard to join them again. He hadn't harmed Sherra, after all, but had managed to let her get away.

Even so… Brody asked Michael about him. Mike claimed the guy was legit, a longtime trusted player who was remorseful. He'd been careless, sure, but had learned his lesson.

Brody still wasn't one hundred percent confident, but surely the guy would be on best behavior—and full alert—if called in again.

"Okay, assume I'll be there. I need to make a couple of calls first, and I'll let you know if something changes, but—"

"No buts. No changes. Be there tomorrow." Michael hung up.

Irritated, Brody slipped his phone back in his pocket, then tried to loosen up before turning toward Sherra again.

She stood near the window, looking out over the view—not much in this dismal location surrounded by the lights of other seedy motels, restaurants and gas stations.

He joined her, pulling her back slightly to be less visible, backlighted by the low illumination in the room.

"What's going on?" she asked.

"I've got to go back to AFD tomorrow." He knew his irritation reverberated in his tone. "I'll call Roy to come here to keep you company."

To his surprise, she didn't disagree. Instead, she said, "Here. I've got something to show you." She still had "Bobby's" phone in her hand, and held it out so he could see the screen.

Just phone numbers, as he'd been reviewing before.

But he immediately recognized what she wanted to show him.

"Damn," he said, taking the instrument from her and scrolling once more toward the end of the numbers.

He didn't know who they belonged to.

But several of them sported the area code and first three digits indicating they were numbers stemming from offices at the Pentagon.

Chapter 17

Sherra saw the dismay and anger on Brody's face, although he didn't say a word. She didn't give him time.

Instead, she began explaining the compromise she wanted. "This whole thing has gotten so complicated, yet if you'd let me work on my computer on my own I might be able to dig out some of the answers you want—like who these numbers belong to."

"I can just call them." He stood rigidly beside her as he stared at the numbers he moved up and down the screen.

"And give yourself away—even if you use some neutral phone to call from. Look, here's the deal. If you let me do some research, I'll stay right here and even let Roy hang around to bother me if you want."

She waited for Brody's explosion, watching him. His hand tensed on the phone, as if he prepared to hurl it. The amber of his eyes darkened as though tensing for a storm. But then he looked directly at her.

"You'll stay here till Roy arrives? And then you'll stay with him till I get back?"

"You'll return here after your regular workday at AFD?"

He nodded. "As long as I'm sure I'm not followed or otherwise hijacked. But you'll also keep in touch. I'll give you back your phone." His scowl deepened. "No, that won't work. You can't turn it on, in case there's a chip in it that they can use to track you."

She didn't like his use of the amorphous, unidentified "they" but knew what he meant. She had to ask—even goad him—though. "But can't they track me by way of my computer? That's how you found me in the first place, isn't it?"

"Not exactly. The fact you were hacking into sites that didn't concern you put you on the radar of the very diligent IT folks who assist the department I'm working for. They were able to trace your identity from that, but not your location. Not directly. They figured out who you were, where you worked and where you live through normal channels, not a chip or GPS."

"So even though they know who they're looking for now—lucky me—the fact we're still using different IDs means they won't know to look for us here?"

"That's the intent and it should be fine, at least for you. Your use of your new ID has been limited and it's not connected to our location. Even so, we still need to be cautious." He paused, his eyes staring so deeply into hers that she felt almost mesmerized. "So we're in agreement? I'll call Roy to come stay with you tomorrow, and you'll do whatever you can to track the origins of phone numbers and destination of emails on your computer."

"Yes, we're in agreement." She smiled. "Now, let's seal the deal."

Bad idea? Maybe. But one of these nights was going to

be their last together, and Sherra wanted to enjoy his presence all she could until then.

She pulled the curtains shut behind him, gently removed the phone from his hand and pulled him down for a hot kiss she planned for him to remember all day tomorrow…and thereafter.

Sherra heard Brody's breathing deepen as she lay beside him. She savored the fact that he was still so near. That their lovemaking had, yet again, been so intense. So wonderful.

So unforgettable.

She would need to live with that soon. Things couldn't keep on as they were.

Especially since she felt confident of her own search abilities. While he was gone tomorrow, doing whatever he did working undercover as Jim Martin, she would find at least some of the remaining answers he needed.

Then, after Brody did what he had to and brought the killers to justice, he wouldn't need to be around her any longer. His sense of military duty would again prevail.

Her eyes closed, and she let her mind wander up and down her body, savoring in her mind all she had just experienced again.

Brody, hot and incredibly sexy and, for what was probably the final time, hers.

She put on a cheerful face as he kissed her goodbye behind the still-closed motel room door.

They had already gone out to a nearby dive for breakfast, and she'd brought back a large cup of coffee to caffeinate her mind and keep it stimulated—not really necessary. Her computer research would do that.

"You'll keep in touch with me," he reminded her, holding her hand and staring into her eyes.

She had already shown him that she had her own cell phone with her—one the criminals after them wouldn't know about. Brody had accepted that and laughed about her ingenuity. This time.

"Yes," she said softly. "And I'm to stay here and open the door only for the maid and for Roy, who should be here in about an hour." Brody had called Roy and he had promised to get on his way from Glen Burnie soon. "And I'm to identify the numbers on Bobby's phone that appear to be from the Pentagon, and I'm to ease my way into the AFD email system and figure out who the muckety-mucks there have been corresponding with—and download any messages that are relevant to show you later."

Carefully, of course, through unidentifiable back doors since Brody believed the correspondents at the other end could be working for the military or someplace else in the U.S. government.

"Most of all," Brody said, holding her close and leaning his muscular body against the entire front of her, "you're to be—"

"Careful," she finished as his mouth met hers once more.

Brody wasn't used to worrying much, just doing. And dealing with consequences later.

But that was regarding things about himself.

Right now, he was damned worried about Sherra.

He needed to get up and moving again, not just sit at his desk at AFD. But there were a lot of emails that had come in while he was gone that he needed to deal with in his capacity as human resources peon—more resumes, plus follow-ups from people who had applied before.

It wouldn't look good if he accomplished nothing today that someone who had his position for real would get done. So far, no one here had acted as if his cover was blown, so neither would he—although he'd remain cautious. For now, he plowed through at least some of the data.

Upon arriving at AFD about an hour ago, he had used his prior absence and feigned illness as an excuse to walk around the office facility, greeting people and claiming to want to catch up with all that had happened while he recu perated from his supposed cold. He saw who was around and asked about pending projects, especially those in other countries—mostly Afghanistan.

There was, in fact, an upcoming bid on a teardown and replacement of a bombed-out police station.

Brody wondered if it had been a make-work project initiated by the SOBs at AFD who had not wanted Lt. Brody McAndrews to look too deeply into the other ongoing projects in that country and had subsequently killed him. Or so they believed.

Despite all he was doing here, his mind never strayed from Sherra for long. He wondered how she was doing. If she had found anything helpful yet in her hacking on her computer. Whether Roy was already hanging out with her in that small room—with its bed in the center—as he should. A thought that Brody hated, but where else could he go and still keep her safe?

His cell phone rang, and he pulled it from his pocket. Speak of the devil… "Yeah, Roy," he said after pushing the button to answer.

"Where is she?" Roy demanded with no preamble.

Brody's blood turned as icy as a midwinter Alaskan river. "What do you mean?"

"I'm at the hotel you said, and I finally got someone to let me into the room with the number you gave me. It's empty."

Damn the woman! Why couldn't she keep her promises, especially those intended to keep her safe?

"I'll get back to you," Brody spat through gritted teeth,

then pushed the button for Sherra's personal phone—the number he'd communicated with a couple of times while on the road and just after he had arrived here. All had been fine then.

Of course he had no way of knowing where she was speaking from.

"Oh, Brody," her voice whispered a moment later. "I was going to call when I knew what to do. Right now...I'm afraid to say where I am in case someone is eavesdropping after all."

"What do you mean? Sherra, I told you to wait for Roy, that he would protect you. So what—"

"That's why I got out of there, Brody. When I started researching the unidentified numbers that Bobby had called, I discovered something I'm sure you didn't know."

"What's that?"

"There was something really odd about one. There was no name attached to it but there was another phone number. Roy's."

The swearing that came from the other end of the phone line was no surprise to Sherra. Brody had always been reasonably good at maintaining his temper, but when he lost it, he never held back on making that known.

"Where the hell are you now?" he finally demanded.

She didn't answer but was already several miles from the hotel. She had been careful, walking a short distance, then hailing a cab to carry her to one large tourist attraction. Then she caught a different cab to somewhere else.

At the moment, she was in the visitors parking garage of the Walter Reed National Military Medical Center in Bethesda. So were a lot of other people, both coming and going. She felt invisible in the crowd—as long as she appeared to be heading toward, or away from, a nonexistent vehicle.

"Here's what I want you to do," Brody was saying. "Don't phone anyone else, but walk to the nearest coffee shop and have them call you a cab." He must think she was still near the hotel. She wouldn't disabuse him of that. Not yet. "Then—"

"For someone who's so cautious, and with good reason considering all we've been through, you talk too much. I'm not discussing over even a probably secure phone what I'm doing or where I'm going—not now. Not till I've figured it out myself. But I promise I'll be in touch…Jim." She quickly hung up.

Did Roy know she had her own cell phone? What about anyone else the false Andrewses might have been in contact with? She'd used it only recently to call Brody but she maintained an account with a major company, so it wasn't impossible for someone to find her number.

That meant the possibility of their learning her location.

Her options seemed few, but she had to do something.

What about hiding in plain sight?

She knew of a place with reasonable security. A place where she'd be welcomed. Maybe even protected, at least a little—although she didn't want to endanger anyone there.

But it would be just for today, until she figured something else out.

Taking a deep breath in resignation and determination, she again pulled out her phone and pushed in a number.

"Hi, Miles," she said when her sweet coworker at CMHealthfoods answered. "It's Sherra. Could I ask you a favor?"

Brody had taken an early lunch break at AFD.

Now, walking down the busy D.C. avenue toward the

nearest shopping center, Brody made the call he'd wanted to for the past half hour, ever since hearing from Roy, then Sherra.

"It's me, Michael," he said to his commanding officer. "We've got a problem."

He filled Michael Cortez in on what had been happening—his leaving Sherra alone because Roy was supposed to come and take care of her, followed by the revelation Sherra made about Roy's phone number indirectly within Bobby's call list.

"Damn." Brody heard a noise that sounded as if Michael had driven his fist through something at his Pentagon office. "Do you know where Roy is? Sherra?"

"Neither. I tried calling Roy again to tell him to stay at the hotel till I got there, but he didn't answer. I'm afraid he's out looking for Sherra. You assured me he's one of ours, always reliable except for that one mistake." Brody had come to trust the judgment of his C.O. before. But now, with Sherra's safety in the balance... "Do you have ways of finding him?"

"Sure do. Via his phone, for one thing. Other ways are too classified to tell even you. I'll get a team on it and keep you informed."

Brody hung up. That was all well and good, but Sherra was in trouble again. This time, it was his fault—more directly than other occasions lately.

And he didn't know where she was.

He called again and was glad when she answered. "Don't give any specifics, but I need to know if you're okay."

"I am—or at least I will be soon. Don't worry about me, Jim. I'll stay in touch. But please don't call again."

She hung up, and Brody stood on the sidewalk arguing with her mentally since he couldn't do it verbally.

He was worried. Sherra had become his secret weapon

in attempting to finally get all the information he needed. Or she would be if she were in a safe haven somewhere and able to work.

If anyone knew that, she would be in even more danger.

And that was far from the only reason he worried about her.

He would call her again.

First he needed a plan of action.

"So where have you been? Really, I mean." Miles glanced at Sherra from the driver's seat of his compact car. "With that guy Jim?" He shook his head. "I told you he was no good. Did he dump you?"

"We dumped each other," she said, annoyed at Miles's attitude. "How are things at work? Does anyone miss me? Did you cover for me?"

Her turn to put him on the defensive. Not that he owed her anything.

"I think I did a great job. Everyone expected you back yesterday after the weekend, but I said I'd heard from you and you were still sick."

It was hard to believe that it was only Tuesday, and the last time Sherra had been at work was the previous Wednesday. "I appreciate it, Miles," she said. "A lot."

They reached the CMHealthfoods building and Miles pulled into the parking lot. Despite her preference to wear business clothing to work, she was glad that the company dress code was relatively lax except when important meetings were scheduled. Otherwise, her gray slacks and black knit top would feel much too casual to be here.

Even so, it took Sherra a little time to get into the building since she had to claim she'd lost her ID due to a theft, and she couldn't even show her driver's license. Not when the only one she had identified her as Sally Bradshaw.

But she received a new company identification card relatively quickly, thanks to her photo and other info being in company computer files.

She felt even more relieved when she reached her office and not only Phoebe, her secretary, fawned all over her, but even her boss, Vic, acted pleased to have her back.

She only wished she truly was in a position to take her entire life back—without worrying about her safety. Or Brody's. But she still had no idea even what she would do that evening.

And she hadn't a hope of trying to catch up with her real work that day. Not when her first priority had to be getting on the computer and extracting, once and for all, the information Brody needed to catch whoever at AFD and otherwise had set him up to be killed.

Only when that was behind her—and no matter how sorry she would be when Brody was out of her life—could she truly be herself once more.

She sat at her desk in her small office and logged onto her computer with the fake info she had put together previously, when she used her lunchtimes and after-work hours to dig into what might have happened to soldier Brody McAndrews.

And then she got to work on hacking into the upper echelon emails at All For Defense.

Chapter 18

After all this time, Brody believed he knew how Sherra thought. Maybe.

With so much of the puzzle of AFD, its government contacts and who knew what about him still unsolved, he hated to leave his post again but had no choice. Not with Sherra in danger once more.

Her safety trumped everything. He had to find her.

Brody grabbed tissues from a box on a shelf in his office and hurried to Crandall Forbes's office. Knocking on the half-ajar door, he poked his head in and managed to sneeze onto a tissue—as always, not hard thanks to the smell of cigarette smoke.

"Sorry, Crandall," he said, glad he was close to perfecting his assumed nasal voice after all these episodes. "I'm having another relapse." He coughed once more to add to the effect. "I need to go home and rest."

"Get over it this time," his thin, homely boss grumbled,

shooting him a sneer that made it clear that Jim/Brody's days here would be numbered otherwise. "And get back here fast."

"I'll try," Brody whined, hating to act so wimpy but knowing he had no choice. And then he was gone.

He believed Sherra would go somewhere familiar. He doubted she'd be foolish enough to head for her home after being attacked there, but she might pop in long enough to throw more clothes into another suitcase so she could deal with disappearing more comfortably. He went there first.

She wasn't around. There was no indication that she'd been home. He saw nothing out of place, and her closets and drawers still had clothes in them.

As he left, he called the CMHealthfoods offices to see if she might be there. He was routed to Phoebe, Sherra's secretary whom he'd met before when he visited.

"Sherra?" Phoebe chirped. "I don't think she's here, but who's calling, please?"

"Jim Martin." That was the ID he had used there before.

"Just a moment." He was put on hold, which riled him as he drove as fast as he dared on crowded roads toward the facility. But it probably wasn't more than a minute before Phoebe returned. "Sorry, she's not here. Would you like to leave a message?"

"Just ask her to call me." That wouldn't happen. The tone of Phoebe's professionally firm but grandmotherly kind voice suggested she was doing as she'd been told and lying.

Or maybe Brody just hoped that so since he had few ideas about where to find Sherra.

When he hung up, he concentrated again on driving— more or less. His mind kept leaping into Sherra's office and whether she would be there when he arrived, or whether she would already have fled. Again.

* * *

Sherra waited for a minute after Phoebe buzzed her, but apparently Brody had bought the idea that she wasn't around. Good thing Phoebe asked no questions when told to tell anyone who inquired that Sherra wasn't there.

Now, Sherra felt soothed by the clicking rhythm of her typing as she sat at her desk staring at her high-resolution computer screen.

She smiled, even as she reached roadblocks in her searches.

They were challenges, and she loved challenges.

Her job was fun because she searched the globe for CMHealthfoods' competitors' promotions and other information, but this was even better.

There it was—the next roadblock that prevented her from sidling into the email system of the highest pooh-bahs in the AFD hierarchy. She studied it for a moment, then typed in her next avenue to circumvent security.

At the same time, she used all the techie wizardry within her knowledge to hide not only that someone was penetrating parts of the system, but also, in the event that information was nevertheless figured out, disguising who it was.

She kept her ears on alert as she remained in her office, door closed. She still had no idea what she was going to do, where she would go later.

Her only idea was far from ideal, but for one night she could allow Miles to be her knight in shining armor, a position he seemed to crave. She could say she'd lost her credit cards which, in a way, was true—or at least her ability to use them freely. She could tell him there'd been some odd vermin within her condo complex, so she didn't want to stay there that night. In a way, that, too, was true. The creep who had attacked her was certainly less appealing than the lowest rodent imaginable.

But Miles would undoubtedly believe he had finally penetrated her female defenses and that she was, at last, attracted to him.

Poor Miles.

No man could compete, in mind, and certainly not in body, with Brody-Jim-Bill.

Especially not this soon after their last, utterly amazing, physical exercises. The memories even now, while she was hard at work, started heating and swirling inside her, and she let them. Too bad it hadn't been romantic bonding, as well.

But even if they finally found the criminals and Brody was able to—

What was that?

Sherra stared at the screen. The great, amazing and altogether exciting thing, the thing that proved her incredible capabilities on the internet, was that she had finally gotten past what appeared to be the last obstacle preventing her from reading all AFD email in their entire system.

The scary thing was what she'd found.

She plugged in her thumb drive to copy the most important correspondence she had located.

Maybe she wouldn't hang out with Miles that night after all.

She hadn't planned on getting together again with Brody, but he needed to see this. She pulled her phone out of her purse and turned it on, then dialed Brody's number.

"Where are you?" he demanded without even saying hello.

"Hi to you, too." But she didn't want to act too cute. "Brody, I did get into that…information you were looking for. There's something you need to see. I can't just tell you about it because you'll want verification. But—"

"Where are you?" he asked again.

"At my business office." Was it okay to say that? What

if someone was listening? She didn't intend to stay here long, but if anyone who shouldn't have had heard what she'd said and interpreted it correctly, she could be toast if they found her.

"Good. I'm just walking up to the security desk. Tell the guys there that I'm okay to come upstairs."

Damn.

Brody had learned through hard experience to be leery, but this was one situation that he'd had not even an inkling of suspicion about. Especially not after all he'd gone through when recruited for this undercover work, when he'd trusted no one, not without proof of reliability.

"Tell me how you got this." He sat on a hard-backed chair beside Sherra in her tiny CMHealthfoods office, looking over her shoulder toward her computer.

The expression on her lovely face was wry as she glanced sideways toward him, and no wonder.

She pushed her straight black hair behind her ear and squinted at the screen as if trying to see past it into the intricacies of the internet. She pursed her full lips in a manner so unconsciously sexy that it made his body react, then she turned back to him. "If you were a techie, I'd explain. But it was pretty complicated to ease my way through the really tight security system in place at AFD—and the fact that it was enhanced because of its Department of Defense contacts made it even dicier." She kept her voice low, even though they were behind closed doors in her tiny office. He appreciated that, for her protection as well as his.

Her coworkers—and bosses—didn't need to know she'd been working on non-CMHealthfoods business on what was supposed to be company time.

Especially because the type of online research she'd

been conducting could jeopardize the whole company if CMHealthfoods was discovered as the source of a leak.

He wanted to hug her for her courage and her intelligence and her apparent success, even as he wanted to punch out the person she had outed with her efforts.

"You're sure about this?"

"I can't guarantee one hundred percent accuracy," she snapped back. "But if you trust me, you'll trust this. The way I got to it was close to foolproof, and I really stuck my neck out. If anyone ever traces it back to me, I could wind up in federal prison for the next millennium. But you know that. You've threatened me with it enough." Her voice had dropped to a frightened whisper.

"That won't happen," Brody assured her. "I've got contacts who'll be very interested in seeing this. Can you copy it?"

She nodded. "Onto the flash drive." She pointed to one that was already connected to her computer.

"Good. Go ahead, then you and I have someplace to go."

She shook her head. "Yes to the first part, but now that I'm here I have to do some real work. I want to come back to my job when this is all over." She paused. "Assuming I'm not in that permanent lockup."

She typed on the keyboard for a few seconds, and he could see on the screen that she was uploading what was there onto the flash drive.

Good.

What she had found changed everything. Or at least everything concerning him, and his assignment, and what he should do next.

The information staring at him from the computer screen showed a bunch of emails from the highest execs at All For Defense. These particular ones were all about projects in Afghanistan.

The projects he had been looking into while he was there, before he had been "killed."

As he had suspected, the roadside bomb that had gotten the other Brody instead had, in fact, been intended for him, Brody McAndrews.

The people at AFD knew he'd uncovered enough irregularities in those projects to indicate a lot of shoddy workmanship at U.S. taxpayers' expense.

Worse, AFD's poor showing was known within the Department of Defense. Condoned by it. Not by everyone, of course, but by those who'd been bribed to look the other way.

All that had been within Brody's suspicions. What he'd needed to do was to prove it, and these emails would finally do that. His undercover work here, in the States, for AFD, might actually be drawing to a close.

The problem was, he needed to determine how to handle what he'd learned. What he now could prove.

He was used, in the military, to going up the chain of command. It was what had been drilled into him.

But what was on the damned screen, in the emails that Sherra had uncovered, was a significant person within the DOD who'd been accepting bribes and hiding the truth. The one who'd been so afraid of being found out that he had manipulated Brody's intended death. And then, he had helped to set things up to hide which Brody had actually been killed so the survivor could go undercover to ostensibly learn the truth.

While being manipulated every step of the way.

The Army Corps of Engineers? Hell, maybe they were involved, too, as Brody had originally believed—and been told. But these indicated that the highly vetted government contracts arm of the Department of Defense hadn't been so highly—or accurately—vetted after all.

Over these weeks, Brody had considered many scenarios,

many possible perpetrators who'd been behind the explosion meant to kill him. But one person he had eliminated each time his possible involvement had come to mind, particularly thanks to his trust in the government contracts arm of the DOD, was the one who'd been guilty after all.

It was Brody's commanding officer, Captain Michael Cortez.

Chapter 19

The steakhouse where they were to meet Ragar was, like last time, in Crystal City, Virginia, not far from the Pentagon and within the underground shopping and restaurant area.

Now, Brody and she sat at a corner table in the dimly lit establishment, waiting. Again. This place held the aroma of well-broiled steaks and there were softly burning candles on each table.

"You're sure you can still trust Ragar?" Sherra whispered. Brody was clearly upset that one of the people he had trusted, his superior officer, had been outed as an enemy.

Brody shrugged. "I think so, but who knows? I'd no reason to mistrust Cortez—none I was aware of. Till now."

"Ragar apparently didn't know the truth about the false Andrews family when we met with him before," Sherra reminded him. "That might be in his favor."

"Right. And he's now actively involved in their prosecution. As he will be with Michael's, I'm sure."

"Then we can trust him?" Sherra asked in confirmation.

"Sure. For now. There he is."

Brody nodded his head toward the door, where Ragar, tall, thin and again dressed in a suit, had just walked in and was leaning down to speak with the maître d'. The greeter must have told him where to find them, since he turned and strode between the mostly occupied seats toward them.

Brody stood immediately. He was still dressed in his button-down shirt and slacks, but again wore no jacket or tie to meet this more formally dressed man.

Even so, Sherra felt terribly underdressed in her casual gray slacks and black knit top.

Once more, Ragar shook hands quickly. "Hello, Ms. Alexander. McAndrews."

Sherra smiled wryly as she sat back down. The two men were already engaged in conversation, practically ignoring her.

They kept their voices low, but Sherra heard Captain Michael Cortez's name mentioned, then hers. Brody nodded toward her, and Ragar glanced in her direction. "I was aware that you were looking into matters online before, and breaking into sites that didn't concern you, Ms. Alexander, but Brody is such an integral part of our operation that we allowed him to deal with you and get you to stop. Good thing he decided to use your services instead. It appears you've turned into an asset—assuming that what you found is true and Captain Cortez is playing the role of a double agent."

The server came to take their drink orders, seconded by an assistant who put a basket of rolls on the table. Ragar and Brody ordered gin and tonics. Sherra decided on a glass of beer.

When the server had left again, Sherra discovered that Ragar's eyes, light blue and glowing in the candlelight, were once more focused on her. She didn't remember any question pending, but his expression suggested he was studying her for an answer. She smiled faintly, not at him but at her own hand as she picked up a roll and a pat of butter.

"Brody explained in general how you learned about our possible traitor, Sherra, but I'd like to hear it from you." He'd used her name for the first time. Did that mean he finally trusted her?

But possible traitor? "I'll tell you some of it, John. What I found made it clear that emails were going back and forth from the executives at All For Defense and Michael Cortez, and they weren't just talking about the weather. There's obvious corruption going on there, and worse. The AFD guys were looking to continue making a fortune from the U.S. and were willing to pay a percentage of it to someone who could help throw business their way. They were also willing to protect him along with their own shady operations." Sherra glared at Brody. Hadn't he already passed this along to Ragar?

"You already know from our previous discussions, John, how good and dedicated—and accurate—Sherra can be on the computer," Brody said. His tone was placating, but his expression harbored no doubt as he regarded his boss with a hard expression in his amber eyes.

Which stoked Sherra's feelings of warmth. He was sticking up for her. Protecting her, in a way. Making it clear to this high-ranking civilian that he believed in her.

"I don't dispute that," Ragar said. "And I have some agents I trust looking into these allegations, and into everything Cortez has been doing over the past year or so. But he's a member of our team."

And Sherra wasn't. That was his implication. In fact, she had been a thorn in their side ever since she started trying to learn the truth about Brody.

She doubted Ragar liked her much. She didn't care—

but she didn't necessarily want to stay on his bad side. That could be harmful to Brody. Not to mention her, if he wanted to roll the weight of the government against her.

"I understand how you want to be sure," she said. "I know Brody trusted the man. In some ways, I'd like to be wrong." But she knew she wasn't.

Not unless Captain Michel Cortez was being framed by someone....

That possibility had entered her mind before. This man could certainly ferret out the reality. But if Cortez was being framed, who might be doing it? The why was obvious: to protect him or herself.

Their dinner was served, and for a while Sherra ate small bites of steak as if she had an appetite, and eavesdropped as the men spoke about what Brody had been doing, and all he had learned, at AFD.

At first she felt good about it, as if she had finally been accepted by Ragar.

But then she began to wonder. As she listened to Ragar discuss who at AFD was undermining the work being done by the company for the U.S., and how Brody could prove it, she was struck by his quiet and composure and acceptance.

As if he was humoring Brody.

What if he disagreed but wasn't about to let his underling on the front lines know about it?

The underling who might be in danger if all wasn't as he now believed.

Did Ragar know more about Cortez than he was letting on?

What if Brody's lukewarm response when Sherra asked if he still trusted Ragar was right? Could Ragar be conspiring with Cortez?

Framing him?

Or was Sherra simply paranoid because of all she'd been through? They'd been through?

But in case this man was picking Brody's brain in order to explode it, and him, for real this time, Sherra knew she had more research to do.

She glanced at Brody. He must have felt her gaze, since he also looked at her. There was a caring look in his eyes. And a quizzical one, as if he wondered what she was thinking.

And damned sexy, even if this wasn't the time or place to think about that.

Or how it would feel if she was wrong and he got so mad that he never wanted to make love with her again.

Brody accompanied Ragar, edging between tables toward the sign indicating the restrooms' location. But taking a leak clearly wasn't on the man's mind.

He obviously wanted to go somewhere to talk to Brody without Sherra's presence.

Which was fine with Brody. She'd been a huge help. Definitely a valuable asset despite the initial problems she had caused for him.

But what she had found changed a lot for Brody. Even with Ragar's backing, protecting her might be a lot dicier now, especially if anyone even hinted to Captain Cortez why he was now under suspicion of murder and bribery. He undoubtedly had allies—unidentified and potentially dangerous. Only in the government? At AFD? Most likely both.

Brody would sound out Ragar, see what kind of help he'd provide. If any. Right now, Brody wasn't inclined to rely on anyone. Let alone trust them.

"Okay," Ragar said quietly. They were at the far end of the hall where the restrooms were located, near an exit door. "We need to set a trap for Captain Cortez. I didn't want to say anything in front of Ms. Alexander, but so far what she's supposedly learned by her hacking—even with all those email messages she's downloaded—I've had some guys looking into it, and it smells. Not that I'm blaming her." He held up his hand, and Brody realized his protectiveness of Sherra must be written in his expression. "But she's found what someone might have wanted to be found. We may be able to use her assistance to figure it out, but I don't want her to know about it."

That was the opposite of what Brody wanted to hear. He intended to get Sherra out of the middle of all that was going on, as quickly as possible. "I think it would be better if we sent her to a new safe house, without her computer. If Cortez, or whoever is behind framing him, figures out that she was the source of the information, she may not survive it this time. She's a civilian, and she's outlived her usefulness to us. Let's just get her out of it."

"I'll consider that," Ragar said. "But this operation is taking a lot longer than I wanted it to." He glared at Brody, obviously blaming him. "She at least set us on a trail that might finally end it." He paused. "Although I'll want her to keep quiet about that. For our ongoing security and future effectiveness, I'll want to deal with our own ineptitudes without letting our team members know they were outsmarted by someone who had no business being involved at all."

Brody caught himself before he smiled. He'd have some leverage here to protect Sherra. "That should work. But for now, I want to be at AFD while this plays out. I want to see the execs there squirm, and what they squirm over, as Cortez's possible treason is revealed."

"Fair enough. I'll work out a new safe house for Ms. Alexander. In fact, I've got someplace in mind, and a couple of highly trusted members of the military police to protect her. Your buddy Roy Bradshaw, by the way, is in custody being interrogated. He may be a resource for figuring out the truth about Captain Cortez. For now, though, excuse me for a few minutes." He nodded toward the restroom door.

Brody headed back toward the restaurant area. But when he reached the end of the hall and glanced toward the table, Sherra was gone.

They'd gone to the little boys' room for some male bonding—or quiet and covert conversation—without her. Fine. Sherra got that.

But she was edgy. Irritated. Wanted answers and closure soon.

That was what made her decide to do something that was probably pretty foolish. But if it led to helpful results…well, why not? She'd be careful.

She had gone to the ladies' room shortly after the guys left. Because they hadn't yet paid, she had reassured the waiter that the men in her party had just gone to the men's room. Then she told him she, too, needed to use the facilities. That was obviously more information than he wanted to know, but he had just nodded.

She hadn't spent more than a minute inside the room. Instead, she scoped the area out. A door to the rear hallway was next door. She peeked out there, then stood watching the men's room door from the shadowy entry.

When Brody walked out, heading toward the table, she used her personal cell phone to call Ragar. She'd already jotted down the number for him that she had found on Brody's phone, never knowing when she might want to contact the powers-that-be with jurisdiction over Brody, if she ever believed the level of danger facing him was ramping up and he chose to ignore it.

"It's me. Sherra," she said when Ragar answered. She explained where she was standing. "I've got something I'd like to talk to you about without Brody present. Could you join me for a minute?"

"What's this all about, Ms. Alexander?" he growled.

Sherra ignored the curious look of a woman heading for the ladies' room and stepped farther into the shadows. "Why don't you come find out?"

Before she'd finished her question, there he was. He'd clearly been heading her way even as he interrogated her.

She pushed the door open more and he followed her into a hallway that would have been the restaurant's back alley if it hadn't been in an underground mall.

"So?" he demanded. "What do you want to talk about?"

"A proposition." She looked up into irritated eyes glaring from his narrow face. "I told Brody only part of what I found. There were some threads I followed, emails I read, that made it clear you're part of the AFD conspiracy and cover-up. That you're making quite a bit of money from the bribes they're paying you. If you give me a cut, I'll keep that from Brody and everyone else."

"You're lying," he nearly shouted. "I'm not involved. And if you try to manufacture evidence against me I'll make sure you're in federal prison for the rest of your absurd little life."

He turned and stormed away—but Sherra was interested to see that he headed not for the table, but toward the men's room.

Chapter 20

Brody had listened to the conversation between Sherra and Ragar in shock, his phone pressed to his ear in the moderately noisy restaurant.

What was she doing? Was she nuts?

At least she'd been wise enough to call him and somehow hide her phone so he could hear what was going on. But where were they?

After leaving the restroom, he had returned to their table. He was still the only one there.

He had been concerned when he hadn't seen Sherra. He asked the server if he knew where the woman at his table had gone, and the guy had nodded in the direction from which Brody had come, presumably toward the ladies' room. She must have slipped in there while Ragar and he were engrossed in conversation at the far end of the hall.

Strange that he hadn't noticed her. He always had seemed

to have a sixth sense that told him when Sherra was around and what she was doing while near him.

He'd figured that Ragar's expense account would take care of their meal, so he hadn't touched the check. But now he prepared to throw some bills on the table and go hunt for them.

He glanced up as he saw movement out of the corner of his eye in the direction of the restrooms.

Sherra strode into the dining room and hurried toward him. There was a wry expression on her face, and her lovely brown eyes appeared dismayed.

"You heard?" she asked as she reached him.

"Yeah, I did. What the hell were you—"

Brody noticed Ragar approaching from beyond Sherra. She must have read it on his face, since she stopped talking and turned.

Her expression now bland, and not apologetic in the least, she said, "It was nice seeing you again, John. Unfortunately, I forgot a prior commitment so we need to leave."

Ragar shot Brody a look he couldn't quite read, but it clearly wasn't happy. "Right. Time for all of us to leave, and consider what we to do next to prove or disprove what Captain Cortez is up to. My opinion right now? The poor guy is being railroaded. I'll make sure my staff checks things out carefully. Railroading might be a major pastime around here."

"Right. We'll talk again later, work out what we're each going to do. Sorry." Brody tried to sound placating, but he remained puzzled. Sherra wasn't a kook. What did she have in mind by attacking Ragar that way?

He confirmed that Ragar was paying the check, and they left.

Sherra took his arm as they maneuvered out of the still-crowded restaurant. Once they were outside in the underground hallway Brody tried to stop and ask her again what she'd tried to accomplish, holding her hand tightly.

"I only wanted to narrow our suspect list, Brody. You've got to admit that, when we arrived here, yours included Ragar."

"Yeah, since I don't trust anyone. But if you're wrong this could undermine everything I've been doing. Everything you've accomplished, too. All you've uncovered could now be considered questionable, not genuinely suspicious data seeming to implicate Michael that needs to be checked out."

"Maybe." She sounded both depressed and defiant, and he had to hide the smile that came to his lips. That was Sherra—a highly intelligent bundle of contradictions.

She sped up as if she refused to act even partially glum, even if she felt it. They still held hands, and he let his gait merge with hers.

They turned a corner into another part of the shopping area, toward the parking garage. "Where are we going now?" he asked.

"To the car. I'm ready to leave."

"Know what? Me, too." He also felt frustrated. As if all they'd gone through together had suddenly fallen apart. Would they have to start all over again to try to learn the truth about AFD and its government contacts?

They? Heck, he was going to find a way to ease Sherra out of this, while still protecting her.

They had reached the door to the parking lot and Brody yanked it open. "Look, we've some thinking to do. And planning what's next. For now, to stay safe, we'll go to a hotel tonight. One we haven't used before, in a different area. I'll make some calls tomorrow."

This whole situation remained bizarre, Brody thought. Twisted, convoluted—and dangerous. Especially since all of those he'd considered his best contacts and allies within the government were now either suspects or had reason to hate him—and Sherra.

But then, everything had been bizarre from the time in Afghanistan when he had first believed he'd found evidence specific to AFD's underhanded dealings that seemed even worse than those of other government contractors.

Entering the stairwell, they began their climb to the next level where his car was parked. Unintelligible voices reverberated above them, and when they opened the next door they were met by two couples also using the stairs. The place was busy that night—not bad for their cover, Brody thought.

Tugging on Sherra's hand, he led her toward where he had parked.

He pulled his key from his pocket with his other hand and pressed the button to unlock the doors as they reached the car.

"Hello, you two," said a voice just loud enough to be heard over distant engine noises in the garage. Releasing Sherra's hand, Brody pivoted.

John Ragar was behind them.

And he was aiming a vicious semiautomatic pistol at them.

Sherra gasped as Brody tried to shove her behind him. That wasn't going to happen.

"You're a damned good actor," she accused. "You almost made me believe in your outraged innocence. Brody heard our conversation, too, and he was mad at me, not you."

"You're too astute for your own good, Sherra. My longer relationship with Brody, my superior position to him, made me believe I could keep him in check by using him—and then you came along. I'd be glad to explain what happened and why to you both, but it'd take a while and neither of you has much more time to live. You've both been such damned thorns in my side—you especially, McAndrews, from the time you started poking your nose where it didn't belong in Afghanistan. I had such a nice, lucrative deal going with AFD there. And then when the team sent to dispose of you screwed up so badly and killed your counterpart, I still figured I could keep you in line if I suggested a special operation. My superiors bought into the idea without knowing that my purpose was to keep you under observation and make sure you didn't figure out the truth." He waved the gun toward Sherra. "That was when I inherited you, my dear—and you were more than a thorn. You turned out to be a knife wound because the kind of snooping you did had even larger potential repercussions."

"So you were all about covering your butt by murder in Afghanistan?" Brody sounded disgusted, not at all scared.

"As long as it was done by AFD to cover its butt." He sounded nonchalant, and his aim now seemed fixed on Brody. "Now, take your weapon out and put it on the floor or I'll shoot her right now." He again aimed at Sherra, stepping even closer.

Scowling, Brody obeyed.

Sherra was terrified, more for him than for herself. She knew he would try to shield her. Could she get his gun back?

Why didn't another car go by now, as a distraction? Even a few diners returning to their vehicles would help—although she didn't really want to endanger anyone else.

"Why the hell would AFD protect you?" Brody demanded. "They were paying you, not vice versa."

"Because I had enough hard evidence to bring them down if I wanted—although we'd all be hurt if our little deal became public. The guys at the top who knew I further protected my identity by sending emails from a separate address in the name of a subordinate reporting to me—Cortez—well, they thought it was hilarious."

"You're a traitor," Brody growled. "You and them, too."

"It's all business," Ragar said with a shrug, once more aiming at Brody. "And in case you're wondering, it's expensive paying off the guys dedicated to making sure the whole thing looks legitimate—including our bodyguard Roy and those poor, sad folks, the wannabe Andrewses. Not to mention that masked man I sent. Each of them was instructed to bring dear Sherra in so we could learn what she knew and restrain her—or dispose of her—and they all failed." He looked at Brody. "Really, what AFD's been doing is no worse than any other contractor. If you'd stayed out of it, no one would be hurt—not Andrews, and not your pretty but uncontrolled lady friend." He again waved the gun toward Sherra, who gasped when Brody pushed her aside and took a step toward Ragar.

The gun moved so it was pointed at Brody's chest. "Hold it," Ragar ordered. "I'll shoot you right now if I have to. I'd rather wait, though. If we go somewhere else, you can even delude yourself that you can get control and kill me instead." His grin looked so malicious that Sherra wanted to punch it right off his face. "No matter where we end this, you can be sure I'll set it up to look like a lovers' quarrel between you."

The guy had to be nuts. He was definitely gutsy. They were in a public parking lot, and there he stood, holding a gun on them. He wore gloves, Sherra noticed, so he could leave the weapon after shooting them both, dropping it, no doubt, in a location that would make it appear that Brody shot her, then himself. Or vice versa.

She would never do that. And she hated the idea that, if this man succeeded, the public would undoubtedly believe his terrible scenario of a lovers' quarrel gone wrong.

She had to do something.

Something that wouldn't result in Brody's leaping in front of her again to protect her—and getting shot first.

* * *

"That won't work, Ragar." Brody casually shrugged one shoulder. "The lovers' quarrel bit, I mean. Yeah, we used to be a couple, but that was years ago. Right now, I needed to learn who was ruining my undercover assignment, so I found her. And, yes, in case you're wondering, we did have sex again, a few times. I just took advantage of the situation, that's all."

Sherra would have felt hurt if she hadn't realized that Brody was lying to protect her. Even so, she hated to hear him say it.

He was moving slightly, trying to put himself in the better position to retrieve his gun—or be shot. Again to protect her.

Well, hell, she didn't need protecting. Even if she did, she wouldn't let it happen at Brody's expense.

"You SOB!" she screamed. "What do you mean you just took advantage?" She made sure her voice was loud enough to attract the attention of anyone else on this level of the garage. *Please, if you're there, look without coming close and call 9-1-1,* she thought.

"Shut up!" Ragar aimed the gun at her chest. She froze, and so did Brody. "Now, we're going to get into the car and drive somewhere else to play out the end of this lethal little spat. McAndrews, you drive, and Sherra, you sit in the front seat beside him. I'll be in the back, watching you both." He waved his gun to show he would be more than observing.

Sherra knew better than to get into a car with a potential kidnapper. It wasn't as if there was any question that this man intended to kill them.

At least here they were facing him. He would have total control if he were behind them, able to choose his time to shoot without their having any chance to escape.

"I can't," she moaned softly, then fell to her knees, wishing she were closer to Brody's weapon. "I really feel sick."

"Get up. Now." Ragar's voice was low and so menacing that it seemed to scratch a knife wound into Sherra's vulnerable throat.

She gagged and actually felt her stomach heave.

"I'll take care of you right here, then." He held his gun up, aiming it at her.

Maybe, if he shot her, that would give Brody a moment during the SOB's preoccupation to get control of him, of the gun. To save himself.

"Forget it, Ragar." Brody clearly wasn't thinking the way she was. He moved to plant himself in front of her.

She wouldn't allow it. "No!" she screamed and, maneuvering around Brody, hurled herself toward Ragar.

She heard the gun go off. Did the bullet hit her? She wasn't sure. She plowed straight into the man, knocking him sideways. At the same time, Brody rushed him, his hands clasped into a battering ram as he got Ragar square in the gut, then again on the head.

It worked, didn't it? Ragar seemed to hesitate—enough that Brody slugged him once more, in the jaw. Ragar went down, and Brody dove for his gun.

In seconds he stood, aiming it at the SOB. "It's over, Ragar," he growled.

The man shook his head slightly as he lay, looking somewhat dazed, on the ground. He glanced toward Sherra and laughed.

Laughed?

Only then did Sherra begin to feel pain. She looked down and saw the blood on her chest.

"Yeah, McAndrews. I guess it is over," Ragar said. "Half success is better than none." He laughed again.

And Sherra began to lose consciousness.

Chapter 21

"You're going to be fine."

Sherra, eyes closed, heard Brody's reassurance as if it came from the far side of the parking lot—low and hardly audible.

But she was aware of sirens shrieking nearby, growing closer.

"I know," she asserted, although not as loudly as she'd hoped. The cement of the parking garage was hard against her back. "Don't worry about me. Watch him. Don't let him get away."

"Oh, that won't happen." Assurance dripped from Brody's tone. She opened her eyes to see him standing near her, his muscular frame tense as he aimed the gun downward. She followed it to see Ragar facedown on the cement. She must have lost consciousness since she hadn't seen Brody tie the guy's hands behind his back with what appeared to be Brody's shirt.

She liked the view of his bare, muscular chest as he stood there. The second gun protruded from his pocket.

She also figured she couldn't be too badly hurt since she was so turned on by Brody's hard, sexy appearance.

She glanced around and saw they weren't alone. Bystanders stood nearby. One of them, too, was minus a shirt, and when she looked down at herself she realized that a piece of clothing was fastened somehow against her shoulder. There was blood on it, and the area hurt, but she knew she wasn't dying.

Maybe she lost consciousness again, but when she next opened her eyes it was to see a lot of uniformed cops around, treating the place like a crime scene. She was asked a lot of questions, managed to answer some, and was then put into an ambulance.

"Brody?" she asked.

But he was apparently still being questioned by the cops.

She wanted to be with him. To make sure the authorities understood what had happened. John Ragar was a government muckety-muck, and his story would be different from theirs. Brody'd had the guns last, and the onlookers wouldn't have known what happened.

Were Brody and she in trouble?

Brody strode through the door of the hospital room.

Sherra lay in bed reading a magazine. She looked up, a little pale against the white sheets but otherwise okay. He couldn't see any bandages on her left shoulder since she wore a hospital gown, but he had no doubt she had one beneath the sling that he assumed kept her arm from moving much and aggravating the wound.

"Hi." She looked beyond him at those who had accompanied him. "So, Michael, you're not in jail?"

"No, thanks to you." Brody watched the man who was

still, officially, his commanding officer approach Sherra's bed and bend to give her a hug. He had a thick body, sparse black hair and a round, swarthy face. Like Brody, he wore a white buttoned shirt and dark slacks—semiformal wear around here since they were accompanied by one of the highest-ranking civilians in the Department of Defense. "You do like to get people in trouble by using technology, don't you?" He glanced toward Brody on the other side of the bed and grinned.

"Let's just say I like to use my computer and smart phones," she responded with a smile. "Getting people in trouble is an added benefit." Her gaze wandered until it lit on the stranger beside Michael. "Hi." She held out her right hand, wincing as she moved. Unsurprisingly, her wound must hurt. "I'm Sherra Alexander," she said.

"I know," said the other man, a tall, broad African American dressed in a gray suit. "I'm Kennard Murcia, undersecretary of defense for government contracts."

"Ragar's boss?" Sherra looked at him suspiciously.

"That's right. We're currently conducting an investigation into our procedures and his activities."

"Like shooting me?" she demanded.

"Like allegedly shooting you," he responded, which drew a glare from Sherra.

"What, you think I did it myself? Or that Brody did it? Look, Mr. Murcia, that man has done a lot of damage, including being involved in the attempt on Brody's life that claimed Brody Andrews's instead. And—"

"Conducting an official investigation is a necessary formality, Sherra," Brody said gently, stepping closer and taking her free hand. "But with all the information you've gathered, plus the way it'll lead to other evidence, I'm sure justice will be served."

"Meaning that Mr. Ragar will go to prison for the rest of his life?" She regarded him with a dubious frown.

"If that's where the evidence leads, then, yes," Murcia concurred. "And considering the confrontation you just had with him, and the evidence against Michael, here, that appears manufactured, plus everything else that's been alleged, I think we can assume Mr. Ragar will be charged and most likely convicted of some pretty heinous crimes."

"Like murder and attempted murder." Sherra nodded her head while squeezing Brody's hand more tightly. "And conspiracy with All For Defense, and maybe even treason?"

"Maybe." The undersecretary's smile held both humor and exasperation. "If the facts are as they appear to be, the Department of Defense owes you both an apology and a debt of gratitude."

Sherra seemed to relax, although her grip didn't. "They're what they seem," she affirmed.

She looked tired and fragile, as if all energy had been drained from her by this conversation. "I think we should go now," Brody told the other men.

"Fine," Murcia said. "I mostly wanted us to touch base with both of you to let you know the status of what's going on."

"And to see if I look like some kind of lying witch," Sherra retorted, although her tone was soft, her words slurred with exhaustion.

"You don't," Michael Cortez told her. "And my main purpose for coming was to thank you. We've never met in person before, but despite what you initially tossed at me you may have saved my butt."

Brody hustled them out. When they were gone, he returned to Sherra's room. This ordeal finally seemed to be nearing its conclusion.

It was about time. Brody felt furious, both with the system and himself. He'd been used. Fooled so Ragar and friends could keep an eye on him and control him. Even as he had thought he'd made sure that all people he'd be working with had been vetted.

Problem was, the system allowed them to, in effect, vet and approve themselves. That's how Ragar, who'd been in charge, had hidden his own involvement so well.

Brody had attempted to protect Sherra, since they'd wanted to bring her in, too—and not even that had gone well. At least she was alive.

Now, Brody wasn't certain where his military career would go from here. Where he wanted it to go. But after all he had put Sherra through, and with all the nasty inquiries people who would be defending Ragar were likely to inflict on her, he doubted she would want to keep in touch with him again any more than she had before she'd thought him dead.

The thought of losing her from his life yet again seemed even more painful now than the first time.

"Brody?" came a soft whisper from below him. He looked down.

Sherra's eyes were barely open, but she was looking at him.

"Yes?" he asked softly.

"Will you stay with me?"

"Of course," he said. For today.

But tomorrow, and the tomorrows after that? He doubted that she would want him around when she was herself once more.

And he still had to figure out what was next in his life.

"You're sure you're okay?" Miles hovered around Sherra, who sat at the desk in her office for the first time in more than two weeks.

It was a Monday morning. She had only stayed in the

hospital a couple of days, then had gone home to recuperate. Brody came with her and hung out for a while, but she healed well. Her shoulder remained sore, but she was otherwise okay.

Physically, at least.

Brody had left her life again.

"I'm fine," she reassured Miles, who sat his lanky form down on the chair across from her. "I'm still taking it easy, but as long as I keep my fingers near the keyboard I don't move my shoulder much."

"Good."

She turned to smile at him—a friendly look, but not too friendly.

Even so, he continued, "I'd be glad to drive you home tonight. We can grab dinner. You shouldn't try cooking, even for yourself, for a while." His soft blue eyes were hopeful.

"Not tonight," she said. Guilt surged through her at his sad expression. She didn't want to lead him on, but there wasn't anything between them.

Would never be, even with Brody out of her life.

He had spoiled her for most men. Maybe someday she'd reconsider, but at the moment a new relationship was out of the question—especially with a nice but geeky guy like Miles.

Fortunately, before she had to say anything else, Vic popped into her office, followed by Phoebe. Her tall, heavy boss looked at her from beneath his thick gray brows and said, "I heard you were finally back, Sherra. Welcome. I'll give you this morning to catch up. Come see me at one this afternoon and I'll talk to you about what I want you to research next for CMHealthfoods."

Behind him, Sherra's secretary rolled her eyes. "Now, Vic," she said, "let her ease back into everything gradually. The poor thing has been injured." Phoebe was always the mother hen and Sherra had never appreciated it more than now. She shot a look of gratitude to the middle-age woman who'd crossed her arms over her ample chest.

"Well, come see me," Vic insisted. "You can tell me if I'm pushing too hard."

They all departed her office a few minutes later, leaving Sherra alone with hundreds of unopened emails and her thoughts.

She tried concentrating on her work, but her mind kept returning to her situation. She'd been visited in the hospital by some additional government suits who'd made it clear they knew about her hacking into secure sites—and that she'd better never do that again or there'd be severe consequences. This time they'd let it go because of the useful results.

Her hacking days— at least into government sites—were through.

Mostly, though, she thought about Brody.

And his absence from her life for the past four days that promised to stretch into forever.

She'd expected it, of course. Although the investigation into All For Defense and John Ragar's apparent nefarious affiliation with it continued, Brody's undercover work as Jim Martin was no longer necessary. He was still in the military, though, and about to be assigned somewhere else.

His choice of a career had split them up before. It would again now. She wasn't the same person who'd felt better breaking up with him than not knowing when or if she'd see him next. But they still led very different lives.

With his background, another kind of covert operation was likely. Something he'd never be able to tell her about even if they kept in touch.

Which they had so far—by phone. She didn't know where he was and he hadn't been specific.

Maybe she could have tracked him down using her skills and technology, but she wasn't about to do that. Not now.

She knew he was alive. And if he wanted to remain out of her life once and for all, then so be it.

It was past six o'clock. Sherra hadn't planned on staying at work so late on her first day back, but she'd gotten caught up in her emails.

A good thing, too. They kept her mind occupied.

But she'd eventually left. She had stopped on her way home to pick up dinner. No turkey burger this time, which she thought of, though—and how it reminded her of the night Brody reappeared in her life.

No, this time she had a chicken sub with lots of cheese and lettuce. She would eat it in front of her TV, veg out for as long as she could stay awake, and then head for bed.

Alone. In one of the beds where she had spent some sexy time with Brody that she would always remember.

Unlocking the door to her condo, she hurried down the dimly lit hallway into her kitchen. She gingerly put her handbag onto the seat of a chair, careful not to hurt her shoulder. She had worn a dark green pantsuit with a lemon-colored shirt that was easy to button to work today and hung her jacket on the back of the chair. She kept her flat shoes on.

She considered a glass of wine, then decided against it. It would only make her sleepy faster.

She heard a sound. And froze.

Could it be Brody? But it might be some cohort of Ragar's who'd gotten away and wanted revenge. She'd have to get out and—

"Hello, Sherra." Brody stood in her kitchen doorway, aiming one of his sexiest smiles at her.

Despite the way her heart leaped in delight, she scowled.

"Damn it, Brody, you scared me. Again. Why didn't you call? Or—"

He had crossed the kitchen and pulled her carefully into his arms. He stifled the rest of her complaint by pressing his mouth on hers so hard that it took her breath away. Or maybe it was his kiss that made her nearly faint with pleasure. Or the surge of heat that wafted through her body, settling in her most sensitive areas.

She didn't pull away despite the slight twinge of pain in her shoulder. Instead she pressed closer. Let her lips and tongue duel with his in a kiss full of heat and promise.

Soon, though, he lifted his mouth from hers. She looked up at him, at his angular features and amber eyes that she knew so well.

"What are you doing here?" she managed to whisper, irritated that her tone wasn't harsher. She was angry with him.

Or wanted to be.

"Do you have enough dinner to share with me?" His grin told her he was just trying to rile her some more.

"Only if you give me some answers."

"Okay, how's this one. I'm staying in the D.C. area, probably permanently."

"Really?" Sherra hated that her voice came out in an excited squeal. "I mean, what will you be doing?"

Keeping his arm around her, he led her to the kitchen table and gestured for her to sit down. He did the same, on the chair nearest hers. "I'm about to become Kennard Murcia's gofer, the assistant to the undersecretary of defense for government contracts."

He looked so pleased with himself that she smiled and reached out for his hand. "You're taking Ragar's position?"

"Yep. It looks like he won't be available for a long, long time. Probably forever, if all the charges about to be brought against him stick."

"That's wonderful!" Sherra's mind was reeling. So was her heart. Brody was here, in her condo. He was going to be living in the general area. The Pentagon, near Arlington, Virginia, wasn't very far from Bethesda, Maryland.

"I've already contacted my parents and brother, let them know I'm okay and will be visiting with them here soon. They were pretty happy."

She could only smile at that. Of course they were happy.

"So, I'll need a place to live," he continued, "and I was wondering if you'd want a roommate. The commute won't be too bad from here. I'd be willing to share expenses, of course. And if you're up for it and things work out, someday we can turn it into a permanent arrangement."

"Permanent, like—"

The smile vanished from his face, replaced by something that Sherra had never seen before—a kind of expression that radiated passion and intensity and more.

"Like, I love you, Sherra. I want to marry you, be with you forever."

"Oh, Brody," she whispered, rising to her feet. He did the same.

This time their kiss was softer, less passionate—but full of commitment.

When it ended, she again looked at him. "For once I definitely agree with your plans, Brody McAndrews."

She was chagrinned to see his face fall, if only a little. "One thing I want to do straightaway, now that I won't have to keep my own identity a secret any longer, is to look up Brody Andrews's real family. Visit them, and tell them what happened so that maybe they can get some closure."

"I'll help you find them," she said firmly, "although the information should be readily available through your official Department of Defense records."

"Right."

"I'll come with you, if you'd like. The meeting will be difficult, but maybe I can help."

He drew her even closer, if that was possible. "That's one of the things I love about you, Sherra. You like to dig in and help—even when your help can get you into trouble. Fortunately this time, even though the assignment is sad, it should be safe."

"I hope so. Now, I think you've met your end of our deal."

"Deal?"

"About dinner. Want half a chicken sub?"

"Sounds good. Only, I want to rev up my appetite first with a little exercise." He rubbed against her, and she could feel what kind of exercise he had in mind.

"I like that idea." She moved away, grabbed his hand and led him to her bedroom—for their first night of forever.

* * * * *

REQUEST YOUR FREE BOOKS!
2 FREE NOVELS PLUS 2 FREE GIFTS!

 Harlequin®

ROMANTIC
SUSPENSE
Sparked by Danger, Fueled by Passion.

YES! Please send me 2 FREE Harlequin® Romantic Suspense novels and my 2 FREE gifts (gifts are worth about $10). After receiving them, if I don't wish to receive any more books, I can return the shipping statement marked "cancel." If I don't cancel, I will receive 4 brand-new novels every month and be billed just $4.49 per book in the U.S. or $5.24 per book in Canada. That's a saving of at least 14% off the cover price! It's quite a bargain! Shipping and handling is just 50¢ per book in the U.S. and 75¢ per book in Canada.* I understand that accepting the 2 free books and gifts places me under no obligation to buy anything. I can always return a shipment and cancel at any time. Even if I never buy another book, the two free books and gifts are mine to keep forever.

240/340 IDN FEFR

Name _____ (PLEASE PRINT)

Address _____ Apt. #

City _____ State/Prov. _____ Zip/Postal Code

Signature (if under 18, a parent or guardian must sign)

Mail to the **Reader Service:**
IN U.S.A.: P.O. Box 1867, Buffalo, NY 14240-1867
IN CANADA: P.O. Box 609, Fort Erie, Ontario L2A 5X3

Not valid for current subscribers to Harlequin Romantic Suspense books.

Want to try two free books from another line?
Call 1-800-873-8635 or visit www.ReaderService.com.

* Terms and prices subject to change without notice. Prices do not include applicable taxes. Sales tax applicable in N.Y. Canadian residents will be charged applicable taxes. Offer not valid in Quebec. This offer is limited to one order per household. All orders subject to credit approval. Credit or debit balances in a customer's account(s) may be offset by any other outstanding balance owed by or to the customer. Please allow 4 to 6 weeks for delivery. Offer available while quantities last.

Your Privacy—The Reader Service is committed to protecting your privacy. Our Privacy Policy is available online at www.ReaderService.com or upon request from the Reader Service.

We make a portion of our mailing list available to reputable third parties that offer products we believe may interest you. If you prefer that we not exchange your name with third parties, or if you wish to clarify or modify your communication preferences, please visit us at www.ReaderService.com/consumerschoice or write to us at Reader Service Preference Service, P.O. Box 9062, Buffalo, NY 14269. Include your complete name and address.

HRS11B

Harlequin®

ROMANTIC

SUSPENSE

CINDY DEES

takes you on a wild journey to find the truth
in her new miniseries

Code X

Aiden McKay is more than just an ordinary man. As part of
an elite secret organization, Aiden was genetically enhanced
to increase his lung capacity and spend extended time under
water. He is a committed soldier, focused and dedicated
to his job. But when Aiden saves impulsive free spirit
Sunny Jordan from drowning she promptly overturns his
entire orderly, solitary world.

As the danger creeps closer, Adien soon realizes Sunny is the
target…but can he save her in time?

Breathless Encounter

Find out this August!

plus
**BONUS
STORY
INSIDE!**

Look out for a reader-favorite bonus story included in each
Harlequin Romantic Suspense book this August!

www.Harlequin.com

Werewolf and elite U.S. Navy SEAL, Matt Parker, must set aside his prejudices and partner with beautiful Fae Sienna McClare to find a magic orb that threatens to expose the secret nature of his entire team.

Harlequin® Nocturne presents the debut of beloved author Bonnie Vanak's new miniseries, PHOENIX FORCE.

Enjoy a sneak preview of THE COVERT WOLF, available August 2012 from Harlequin® Nocturne.

Sienna McClare was Fae, accustomed to open air and fields. Not this boxy subway car.

As the oily smell of fear clogged her nostrils, she inhaled deeply, tried thinking of tall pines waving in the wind, the chatter of birds and a deer cropping grass. A wolf watching a deer, waiting. Prey. Images of fangs flashing, tearing, wet sounds…

No!

She fought the panic freezing her blood. And was gradually able to push the fear down into a dark spot deep inside her. The stench of Draicon werewolf clung to her like cheap perfume.

Sienna hated glamouring herself as a Draicon werewolf, but it was necessary if she was going to find the Orb of Light. Someone had stolen the Orb from her colony, the Los Lobos Fae. A Draicon who'd previously been seen in the area was suspected. Sienna had eagerly seized the chance to help when asked because finding it meant she would no longer be an outcast. The Fae had cast her out when she turned twenty-one because she was the bastard child of a sweet-faced Fae and a Draicon killer. But if she found the Orb, Sienna could return to the only home she'd known. It also meant she could recover her lost memories.

Every time she tried searching for her past, she met with a closed door. Who was she? Which side ruled her?

Fae or Draicon?

Draicon, no way in hell.

Sensing someone staring, she glanced up, saw a man across the aisle. He was heavily muscled and radiated power and confidence. Yet he also had the face of a gentle warrior. Sienna's breath caught. She felt a stir of sexual chemistry.

He was as lonely and grief stricken as she was. Her heart twisted. Who had hurt this man? She wanted to go to him, comfort him and ease his sorrow. Sienna smiled.

An odd connection flared between them. Sienna locked her gaze to his, desperately needing someone who understood.

Then her nostrils flared as she caught his scent. Hatred boiled to the surface. Not a man. Draicon.

The enemy.

*Find out what happens next in THE COVERT WOLF
by Bonnie Vanak.*

*Available August 2012 from Harlequin® Nocturne
wherever books are sold.*

HNEXP0812